David Hannay, John Parker Anderson

Life of Frederick Marryat

David Hannay, John Parker Anderson

Life of Frederick Marryat

ISBN/EAN: 9783337415228

Printed in Europe, USA, Canada, Australia, Japan

Cover: Foto ©Raphael Reischuk / pixelio.de

More available books at **www.hansebooks.com**

LIFE

OF

FREDERICK MARRYAT

BY

DAVID HANNAY

——— ——

LONDON
WALTER SCOTT, 24 WARWICK LANE
NEW YORK AND TORONTO: W. J. GAGE & CO.
1889

NOTE.

THE materials for a life of Marryat are scanty, and I have acknowledged my obligation to them in the text. Mrs. Ross Church collected, in 1872, all the surviving knowledge about her father's life—all of it, that is, which the family thought it right to publish to the world. The present little book has no pretensions to be founded on new materials. My object has only been to make the best use I could of already published matter—to tell what story there is to tell in the clearest possible manner, and to add the best estimate of Marryat's work and position in letters that I could supply.

D. H.

CONTENTS.

—•⊢—

CHAPTER I.

CHAPTER II.

CHAPTER III.

CHAPTER IV.

CHAPTER V.

CHAPTER VI.

CHAPTER VII.

LIFE OF
CAPTAIN MARRYAT.

————◦✧◦————

CHAPTER I.

FREDERICK MARRYAT, one of the most brilliant, and the least fairly recognized, of English
novelists, was born in Westminster, on the 10th July,
1792, some seven months before the outbreak of the
Great War. He was the second son of Joseph Marryat,
M.P. for Sandwich, chairman of the committee of Lloyds,
and Colonial Agent for the island of Grenada. His
mother was a Bostonian, of a loyalist family. Her maiden
name was Geyer—or according to Mrs. Ross Church's
life of her father, Von Geyer—and the family is said to
have been of Hessian origin. The Marryats themselves
were a Suffolk stock. In Marshall's "Naval Biography,"
which appeared during Marryat's own life, the novelist is
said to have descended from one of the numerous
Huguenot refugees who settled in the Eastern Counties
during the persecutions of the sixteenth century. The
family version of its history, as given by Mrs. Ross Church,
contains a longer and more splendid pedigree, going
back even to knights who came over with "Richard
Conqueror." These things, though set forth with faith

no doubt, are to be received with polite reserve by the judicious reader. For the rest, whatever the remote origin of the Marryats may have been, they were during the seventeenth and eighteenth centuries very distinctly middle-class people—dissenting ministers, doctors, or business men—manifestly of good parts and industry. Some of them wrote sermons and printed them. Thomas Marryat, the novelist's grandfather, was a doctor and the author of a medical book. His father was, as the places he held show, a prosperous man ; and the future novelist entered the world under fairly favourable circumstances. There was, it is clear, no want of money, and the family were active people with a marked tendency to use their pens.

As no detailed life of Marryat was written until long after his death, when no witnesses were left who could speak with knowledge, there is an almost absolute want of evidence as to the character and probable influence of his family life. If we are to argue from his stories, it was hardly to be called happy. These guides may not be entirely safe, and yet they afford evidence of a kind not to be lightly dismissed. A writer whose pictures of home and school life are habitually disagreeable, cannot have had many pleasant memories of his own to look back on. With Marryat this was the case. In all his earlier stories, and until he became decidedly didactic, and religious, in his later years, he described the relations of parents and children, of schoolboy and schoolmaster, as either indifferent or hostile, or as contemptuous even when affection is not absent. Peter Simple, Mr. Midshipman Easy, and Newton Foster are the sons of men

whom they may like, but cannot respect, of whom two
are maniacs, and one is a harmless imbecile. Their
mothers are either utterly shadowy or repulsive. " Frank
Mildmay," the first and the most autobiographical of his
stories, is also the most destitute of kindliness. Something may be allowed for rawness in the author, and
something for direct imitation of the earlier Smollettian
model. Marryat, too, publicly protested that he was not
the " Naval Officer " of this first story. But, by his own
confession, he put many of the incidents of his own life into
it, and we may safely conclude that what is wholly wanting in the story was not prominent in his own experience.
Now what is wanting is any trace that Frank Mildmay
had the smallest filial regard for his father, or was
conscious of any maternal influence, or thought of his
home life with affection, or of his school as other than a
place of torment. That is not how men write when they
look back kindly on their first years. If Thackeray and
Dickens drew such different pictures of boy and school
life, we know why. It is not necessary to rack the scanty
evidence about Marryat's early years, to find reason for
believing that his father was probably a hard and dry
man of business, whose prosperity never melted the
provincial dissenter quite out of him. Of his mother
there is nothing to be supposed at all.

It is to be noted that although Mr. Joseph Marryat
was a prosperous man, he did not send his sons to a
public school. Frederick and his elder brother (Joseph
also, and not unknown as a collector of, and writer on,
porcelain) were sent to some sort of academy kept by a
Mr. Freeman, at Ponders End. It is an almost universal

experience that the boy who has been at a private school
may remember an individual master with kindness, but
never has any degree of respect or affection for the place
itself. He is not one of an ancient body like the public-
school man, and has nothing in his memory to set off against
the restraint — or in the old hard days the floggings and
hardships of school life. The Wykamite might laugh at
the wash pot of Moab, but what private-school boy would
forgive his master for turning him out to wash in a back
yard? What is inflicted by a public school is inflicted by
the school itself; in a private establishment it is inflicted
by the master, and is a personal wrong. Marryat was no
exception to the rule. His memories of Ponders End
were not of a kind to make him draw cheerful pictures
of school life. That he was far from a model pupil, and
had his share of the cane, has nothing to do with it. He
scamped his work, and forgot it, as many other boys
have done and will do. Not only that, but he was the
cause of scamping in others. Mr. Babbage, who was
for a time his schoolfellow, is the authority for a story
which shows that Marryat was indeed a model young
scamp. Babbage wished to work (it does not appear
whether they called it "sweating" or "greasing" at Ponders
End), and to get up for that purpose with another "swot"
at the absurd hour of three. With intentions which
were only too obvious, Marryat, who was his room fellow,
proposed to join the party. Babbage objected, and
thought to escape the intrusion by the easy method of
not waking Marryat. This answered until the creator of
Mr. Midshipman Easy first bethought himself of drawing
his bed across the door, and then when even the moving

of his bed did not rouse him, of tying his hand to the handle. For some nights Babbage got over the difficulty by cutting the fastening, until Marryat found a chain which could not be cut. Babbage had his revenge. He invented an ingenious machine for jerking the chain, and went on waking his chum repeatedly for no purpose. At last a compromise was made. Marryat joined the good boys for early study, and of course it was not long before others joined too, and then the letting off of fireworks and various noises betrayed the secret. How many of the party were flogged does not appear. Before long Marryat had to be up at six bells in the middle watch on duty too often to leave him much inclination to turn out voluntarily, even for mischief, when he could by any chance get a night in.

It is also recorded of Marryat that he ran away to sea three times, that is, he ran away with the intention of getting to sea, but the end of the adventure was always capture, return to school, and more cane. His great grievance is reported to have been the obligation to wear the clothes which his elder brother had outgrown. The detail seems to indicate a certain narrowness, not to say sordidness, in so prosperous a household as the Marryats', and the aggravation was certainly gross enough to justify the protest. On one of these occa-sions Mr. J. Marryat showed a remarkable weak-ness. He gave the truant money and sent him in a carriage back to school. This error of judgment had a very natural consequence. Marryat slipped out of the carriage, found his way quietly home, and took his younger brothers to the theatre. At last his father came to the very sensible conclusion that the sea was the best place for such a boy. Being a man of some influence and position, he was able to start his son well, on board a crack frigate, and under a distinguished captain. In September, 1806, Marryat entered the *Impérieuse*, captain Lord Cochrane, and sailed for the Mediterranean.

CHAPTER II.

FORTUNE could not have done Marryat a greater kindness than to send him to sea on the quarter-deck of the *Impérieuse*. She enabled him to share in the most stirring work to be done at the date at which he joined the service, and under the command of one the most brilliant of naval officers. In 1806 the war of fleets was over. Trafalgar had broken the heart of our enemies, and from that time forward their squadrons never even attempted to keep the sea. Napoleon built line-of-battle ships in batches, but only to keep them manned and armed, lying idle in port. The English fleets had so completely established their supremacy, that they used the French roadsteads as familiarly as their own. The blockading squadron off Brest anchored in Douarnenez Bay, in sight of the French look-out, and there repaired their rigging or caulked their seams as coolly as if no enemy's fleet were in existence, and they did it with perfect impunity. Admiral Smyth has told how audaciously the Mediterranean fleet was wont to anchor off Hyères in the absolute confidence that the French would never come out of Toulon. Their only chance of service was when the French would be de-coyed out by some particularly audacious frigate, which

2

was sent in to insult them at the very mouth of their
harbour. Then there was a chance that they might be
drawn further than they could go back before the inshore
squadron was upon them. But such breaks in the mo-
notony of blockade were rare. For the most part our
line-of-battle ships were employed in cruising to and fro,
·with intervals of harbour—their officers and crews spent
their lives in drilling aloft or at the guns, and in keeping
decks and metal-work in a condition of faultless cleanli-
ness. That passion for neatness and smartness which
has never left the British navy rose to its height in the
last years of the Great War, and did indeed sometimes
attain to actual mania in the minds of captains and first
lieutenants in want of something to employ themselves
and their men upon.

There was, however, one class of ship which had a fair
chance of active service. The frigates were never, even
to the end, reduced to mere patrolling. It was to them
indeed that fell all the brilliant fighting in the last ten
years or so of the war. The French never altogether
ceased to send forth cruisers which had necessarily to be
pursued and captured. Moreover, there was work to be
done upon the enemy's coasts, convoys to be taken, forts
to be destroyed, privateers to be cut out. After 1808
we were in alliance with the Spaniards, and there was
then no want of chances for enterprising officers to distinguish themselves against the French invaders on the
coasts, particularly in the Mediterranean. The Mediterranean, including the Adriatic, and the East Indies,
were the great theatres of the war until the Americans
struck in.

It was a material addition to his good fortune in being appointed to such a ship, and on such service, that he should have begun under the captain who then commanded the *Impérieuse.* The novelist who was to give the most living of all pictures of the navy at its greatest time could not possibly have met with a better chief. Lord Cochrane, who is better known as the Earl of Dundonald, was, next to Nelson (the master of them all), that one of the naval officers of the Great War who was most distinctly a man of genius. There were others who were brave, able, honourable gentlemen. In pure seamanship many may have been his equals. In a service which included such men as Blackwood, Hallowell, Willoughby, the Captain Hamilton who cut out the *Hermione,* Broke of the *Shannon,* and a hundred other valiant gentlemen, even Dundonald could not hope for a pre-eminence in valour. It may even be allowed that he never, while fighting for his own country, was able to achieve anything so complete, so distinctly what Cortes called a "muy hermosa cosa," a very pretty piece of fighting with a squadron, as Sir William Hoste's little gem of a victory over the French frigates off Lissa. He was not allowed the chance to handle a detachment of ships in independent command. But there was in Dundonald the indefinable something—"those deliveries of a man's self which have no name," that combination of passion and faculty—which makes the man of genius. Whatever he did was done with a burning fire of energy. The fire was not always pure. There was a self-assertion about the man—never base, but always aggressive, a pragmatical Scotch fierceness, a love of hate and scorn, a total inability to keep measure, which can be seen on every page of his Autobiography, and explain why it was that he was always, in our service or out of it, a free lance. He was of the race of Peterborough not of Marlborough. To the highest rank he did not belong, but he was divided in kind from the brave, able, disciplined, but shadowy men, who do the regular drilled work of the world. He was a magnificent, rugged individuality. Even in books he is real as only such men as Nelson and Wellington are real. On those who knew him his influence, even if it only produced repulsion, must have been profound. One so open to impressions, and so able to retain them as Marryat, must have been another man all his life for having known and admired Dundonald. It must be remembered, too, that Marryat saw Dundonald at his best—on the deck of his frigate, and not at the Admiralty or the House of Commons, where he was apt to make himself intolerable by his wrong-headed violence in right, and his inability to see that for the work of the reformer, as for all work, there is a proper time, and a fitting manner which must not be mistaken, under penalty of failure.

The influence which Cochrane had upon Marryat might indeed be demonstrated from his works. The captain of the *Impérieuse* remained his type of what a British officer ought to be. All his frigates' captains who are mentioned for honour have something—and several of them have much—of his first commander in them. That this should be the case in " Frank Mildmay," the first of his books, and to some extent an autobiography, was almost a matter of course. In this book the cruise of the frigate on the coast of Spain is the very service of the *Impérieuse*. But it is equally true of Captain Savage of the *Diomede* in " Peter Simple," and of Captain M—— of the " King's Own." Both are Scotchmen, penniless gentlemen of good descent, officers of boundless skill, daring, and withal judgment. It is on this last quality that Marryat dwells by preference, and it is this which he picks out for special praise in Cochrane. " I must here remark," he says in the private log quoted in Mrs. Ross Church's life, " that I never knew any one so careful of the lives of his ship's company as Lord Cochrane, or any one who calculated so closely the risks attending any expedition. Many of the (*sic*) most brilliant achievements were performed without loss of a single life, so well did he calculate the chances ; and one half the merit which he deserves for what he did accomplish has never been awarded him, merely because in the official despatches there has not been a long list of killed and wounded to please the appetite of the English public." This fondness of the public for a long list of killed and wounded was a favourite subject of half-serious jest with Marryat, and he learnt from others, if not from Cochrane, how a despatch ought to be written in a " concatenation accordingly." It would seem that Marryat had little admiration for the brainless, headlong courage which rushes madly at whatever happens to be in front of its weapon. He would have condemned even with contempt (and Hawke, Nelson, Cochrane, would have condemned with him) such a piece of frantic swash-bucklery as the last fight of the *Revenge*. The men who were daring with judgment, who risked for a reason, who took care to cover themselves as they lunged, and who then went all together, sword, hand, and foot, with the speed of lightning, and with unerring accuracy of the eye which has brains behind it, were his heroes. In any case Marryat would have arrived at these conclusions, but he assuredly did so the sooner, and the more heartily, because for three years he fought under a fighter of this stamp.

Marryat was fortunate in his messmates as well as in his captain. A crack frigate of those days had the pick of the lieutenants' list, and of the "young gentlemen" who were to be the captains of the future. The *Impérieuse* had a particularly good staff, some of them old officers of Cochrane's, and in the midshipman's mess Marryat met comrades who were good fellows, and gentlemen too. He formed friendships which lasted through life, particularly with Lord Napier, and with Houston Stewart.

I have thought it well to dwell at some length on Marryat's entry into the service, because its conditions are of vital importance in his life. Whatever his training had been he would have been a writer. His private log shows that from the beginning he found pleasure in the use of his pen; but had he not been a naval officer he would have been a very different writer, and, more, had he gone to sea in a less happy way, the misfortune would not have failed to have its effects on him. The tamer life of a line-of-battle ship, the tedium of a small craft engaged on convoy, might have driven him back on shore by mere boredom. On board the *Impérieuse* he was able to live his life to the full. There he had three years of active and daring fighting. The impression they made on him was never effaced, and has been recorded by himself. In the private log, quoted by his daughter, he sums up his memories in words which it would be a dereliction of duty not to quote :

"The cruises of the *Imperieuse* were periods of continued excitement, from the hour in which she hove up her anchor till she dropped it again in port: the day that passed without a shot being fired in anger, was with us a blank day: the boats were hardly secured on the booms than they were cast loose and out again ; the yard and stay tackles were for ever hoisting up and lowering down. The expedition with which parties were formed for service; the rapidity of the frigate's movements night and day; the hasty sleep snatched at all hours ; the waking up at the report of the guns, which seemed the very keynote to the hearts of those on board, the beautiful precision of our fire, obtained by constant practice : the coolness and courage of our captain, inoculating the whole of the ship's company; the suddenness of our attacks, the gathering after the combat, the killed lamented, the wounded almost envied; the powder so burnt into our faces that years could not remove it ; the proved character of every man and officer on board, the implicit trust and adoration we felt for our commander; the ludicrous situations which would occur in the extremest danger and create mirth when death was staring you in the face, the hair-breadth escapes, and the indifference to life shown by all—when memory sweeps along these years of excitement even now, my pulse beats more quickly with the reminiscence."

The years of service which thus impressed themselves on Marryat's memory may be divided into three periods. First, a cruise on the coast of France from Ushant to the mouth of the Gironde; then a longer period of active work in the Mediterranean; and finally, a return to the ocean, and the action in the Basque Roads. The young midshipman's first actual experience of cruising was one which was doubtless present in his mind when he wrote the song whereof the chorus tells how " Poll put her arms akimbo," and said, " Port Admiral, you be ——." When the corporal reported to Mr. Vanslyperken that the crew of the revenue cutter were singing this ditty, the outraged commander asked whether it was the Port Admiral at Portsmouth or Plymouth. The officer who was, we may be sure, spoken of by the crew of the *Impérieuse* on the 17th and succeeding few days of November, 1806, in an equally mutinous fashion, was the Port Admiral at Plymouth. According to the custom of Admirals who did not have to go to sea themselves, this officer was exceeding zealous in enforcing the Admiralty's orders to despatch ships to sea smartly. The orders came down for the *Impérieuse* to go to sea, and the Admiral would have them obeyed. Go she must—"The moment the rudder—which was being hung—would steer the ship," as Dundonald says in his Autobiography, and while she had "a lighter full of provisions on one side, a second with ordnance stores on the other, and a third filled with gunpowder towing astern." But the tale should be told in Marryat's words, and not in his captain's:

"The *Impérieuse* sailed; the Admiral of the port was one who *would* be obeyed, but *would not* listen always to reason or common sense. The signal for sailing was enforced by gun after gun; the anchor was hove up, and, with all her stores on deck, her guns not even mounted, in a state of confusion unparalleled from her being obliged to hoist in faster than it was possible she could stow away, she was driven out of harbour to encounter a heavy gale. A few hours more would have enabled her to proceed to sea with security, but they were denied; the consequences were appalling, they might have been fatal. In the general confusion some iron too near the binnacles had attracted the needle of the compasses; the ship was steered out of her course. At midnight, in a heavy gale at the close of November, so dark that you could not distinguish any object, however close, the *Impérieuse* dashed upon the rocks between Ushant and the Main. The cry of terror which ran through the lower decks; the grating of the keel as she was forced in; the violence of the shocks which convulsed the frame of the vessel; the hurrying up of the ship's company without their clothes; and then the enormous waves which again bore her up, and carried her clean over the reef, will never be effaced from my memory."

The frigate had been carried into a deep pool, and rode the gale out at anchor. When daylight came she was found to be inside instead of outside of Ushant— and was got off with no greater damage than the loss of her false keel. But the escape was a narrow one—the adventure must have shaken Marryat rudely into the life of the sea—and have impressed him deeply with the possible consequence of pig-headedness in pig-headed Port Admirals.

The cruise of the frigate on the French coast was not very fruitful in incident, and early in 1807 she was back in port. There she remained for the greater part of the year, while her captain was fighting the battles of the navy in the House of Commons. A general election took place in the spring, and Cochrane, who had sat already for Honiton, stood with Sir Francis Burdett for Westminster. They were elected, and the captain of the *Impérieuse* at once began, or rather returned to, those attacks on abuses in the Admiralty and dockyards which were so uniformly right in substance and wrong in form. It is a pleasing instance of the inability of man to hold the balance even when his own interest is in the scale, that Cochrane never seems to have seen anything wrong in the retention of a fine frigate in port during war in order that her captain (who was drawing full pay all the time) might attend to parliamentary duties in London. Conscious of rectitude, he would have treated the suggestion that he also was an abuse with scorn. According to his own version of the story, told in profound good faith, he did his higher duties as member of the House with such efficiency that the Admiralty decided to confine him to the exercise of his profession in future. At the close of the session the *Impérieuse* was ordered to join Lord Collingwood's fleet in the Mediterranean, and sailed from Portsmouth on the 12th of September, 1807.

In October, Marryat made his first acquaintance with Malta, and the scenes associated with the immortal memory of Mr. Midshipman Easy. He was not to stay there long, for the *Impérieuse* left almost immediately to join Lord Collingwood, who was cruising off Palermo. Soon after, the future describer of so many dashing affairs with boats had an opportunity of seeing one. On the 14th of November (Marryat himself says the 15th), the *Impérieuse* sighted two vessels under the land of Corsica, and, as it was calm, the boats were ordered out to examine them, under the command of Napier and Fayrer.

" As soon," it is Marryat who speaks, "as they were within half a mile, the ship hoisted English colours. The sight of these colours, of course, checked the attack; the boats pulled slowly up toward her, and, when within hail, demanded what she was, for, if an English vessel, she could have no objection to be boarded by the boats of an English frigate. Now, as it afterwards was proved, the ship was a Maltese privateer of great celebrity, commanded by the well-known Pasquil Giliano, who had been very successful in his cruises, and, if report spoke truly, for the best of reasons, as he paid very little respect to any colours ; in fact, he was a well-known pirate, and, when he returned to Malta, his hold was full of goods taken out of vessels, which he had burnt that he might not weaken his crew by sending them away ; and in an Admiralty Court so notoriously corrupt as that of Malta, inquiries were easily hushed up. Although such was the fact, still it had nothing to do with the present affair.

" When the boats pulled up astern, the captain of the

polacre answered that he was a Maltese privateer, but
that he would not allow them to come on board ; for,
although Napier had hailed him in English, and he
could perceive the red jackets of the Marines in the boats,
Giliano had an idea from the boats being fitted out with
iron tholes and grummets, like the French, that they
belonged to a ship of that nation. A short parley ensued,
at the end of which the captain of the privateer pointed
to his boarding nettings triced up, and told them that he
was prepared, and if they attempted to board he should
defend himself to the last. Napier replied that he must
board, and Giliano leaped from the poop telling him that
he must take the consequences. The answer was a cheer
and a simultaneous dash of the boats to the vessel's side.

" A most desperate conflict ensued, perhaps the best
contested and the most equally matched on record. In
about ten minutes, the captain having fallen, a portion of
the crew of the privateer gave way, the remainder fought
until they were cut to pieces, and the vessel remained in
our possession. And then, when the decks were strewn
with the dying and the dead, was discovered the unfortu-
nate mistake which had been committed. The privateer
was a large vessel, pierced for fourteen guns and mount-
ing ten, and the equality of the combatants, as well
as the equality of the loss on both sides, was remarkable.
On board of the vessel there had been fifty-two men ;
with [the] boats fifty-four. The privateer lost Giliano,
her captain, and fifteen men ; on our side we had fifteen
men killed and wounded. Fayrer lost for ever the use
of his right arm by a musket bullet, and Napier received a
very painful wound, and had a very narrow escape—the

bullet of Giliano's pistol grazing his left cheek and passing through his ear, slightly splintering a portion of the bone."

Marryat's version of the story does not agree in every detail with Cochrane's, but in essentials they are at one. Particularly there is no difference of opinion between them as to the character of the Maltese Admiralty Court. In this case it not only refused to allow that the *King George* (Giliano's vessel) was a lawful prize, but it fined the *Impérieuse* five hundred double sequins. That iniquitous court was one of the many abuses Cochrane had to fight in his life.

Here certainly was an experience likely to be useful to the midshipman who was to record it. The fight was a dashing one—a thing well worth seeing in itself, and besides the *King George* privateer so-called, but in fact pirate or little better, with her motley crew of Russians, Italians, Sclavonians ("a set of desperate savages" Cochrane styled them in his despatch), must have introduced him to the lawless, and scoundrelly fringe of the great naval war. From privateer to pirate was at all times but a step, and amid the confusion of the great wars, with the connivance of dishonest Colonial Admiralty Courts, and the tacit consent of some neutrals of little scruple, not a few ruffians were able to flourish,—the plundering, murdering, cowardly camp followers, so to speak, of the great regular naval armaments.

From Corsica the *Impérieuse* went on to Toulon, to report to Lord Collingwood, who was back at his regular blockading station. Thence Cochrane was sent to Malta, and on to the Ionian Islands to command a

squadron then engaged in blockading some French
frigates in Corfu.   Here Cochrane, true to his character,
fell out with another abuse.   When he arrived on the
station, he found that neutral vessels, or even vessels
belonging to our enemies, were allowed to trade with the
island under cover of passes supplied by the officer commanding the English blockading force.   Of course Cochrane seized them, to the wrath of the officer in question,
who consistently enough intrigued against him at head-
quarters.   The captain of the *Impérieuse* was recalled
as being too indiscreet, by Lord Collingwood, apparently
on the mere complaint of the officer whose passes had
been treated with such scant respect, and so lost his one
chance of commanding a squadron on work which he
was eminently fitted to do well.   The story of the passes
(which of course were not given for nothing) must have
been known to every man on board the *Impérieuse*, and,
doubtless, the officer who had such a remarkable idea of
his duties, went, in the course of time, to the making of
Captain Capperbar.   Having made one more place too
hot to hold him, by hasty action, where a little tact and
patience would have enabled him to have his way and to
bring the trading naval officer to book, Cochrane was
employed cruising to and fro till January, 1808, when he
was despatched by Lord Collingwood to the coast of
Spain, where he was to have a longer period of active
brilliant work.

CHAPTER III

WHEN the *Impérieuse* reached the coast of Spain early in 1808, we were still at war with that country. Napoleon had not yet turned his submissive ally into an enemy by that act of brigandage which was the capital error of his life. The war was for us still a "rich war," as Nelson put it—there were still Spanish prizes to be picked up. Cochrane was master of the work to be done. His previous cruise in the *Speedy* had made him perfectly familiar with the Spanish coast. It had also given him an absolute confidence in his power to beat the Spaniards at any odds. On this occasion he had no opportunity to equal the most marvellous of all his feats—the capture of the frigate *Gamo* with his tiny gun-brig the *Speedy*, but he was incessantly active and uniformly successful. The *Impérieuse* hugged the Spanish coast, destroyed isolated forts, sailed into the very ports and marked her prey down coolly, before sending her boats in to cut out the more tempting prizes. In all this stirring fighting Marryat had such share as a midshipman might. The history of it is recorded in "Frank Mildmay," in "Mr. Midshipman Easy," in "Peter Simple." One incident may be re-

corded as a type of the rest. Lord Cochrane learnt that
a certain vessel which he was resolute to take was lying
at anchor in Almeria. He himself, in his "Autobiography
of a Seaman," calls her "a large French vessel, laden with
lead and other munitions of war." Marryat, as quoted
by his daughter, calls her a polacre privateer, and says
nothing of her nationality, but in other respects the
stories agree. The story may now go on in Marryat's
words :

"At daybreak we were well in with American colours
at the peak. [The place, as has been just said, was
Almeria Bay, and this trick of hoisting neutral colours
was a common stratagem of war.] The Spaniards had
their suspicions, but, as we boldly ran into harbour,
anchored among the other vessels, and furled our sails,
they did not fire. They were puzzled, for they could
not imagine that any vessel would act with such temerity,
as we were surrounded by batteries. We had, however,
anchored with springs upon our cables; close to us
within half-musket shot, lay a large polacre privateer of
sixteen guns, the same vessel which had been attacked
by, and had beaten off the boats of the *Spartan* with a
loss of nearly sixty men killed and wounded. On our
other side were two large brigs heavily laden and a zebecque; the small craft were in-shore of us, the town
and citadel about half a mile ahead of us at the bottom
of the bay, the batteries all around us, and evidently
well prepared. Our boats had long been hoisted out and
lay alongside, which circumstance added to the suspicions of the Spaniards; still, as yet, not a gun was fired.

" Lord Cochrane's reasons for running in with the frigate was, that he considered the loss of life would be much less by this manœuvre than if he had despatched the boats, and this privateer he had determined to capture. He did not suppose, nor indeed did any one, that, lying as she was under the guns of the frigate, she would dare to fire a shot, but in this he was mistaken. The boats were manned, and the remaining crew of the *Impérieuse* at their quarters. The word was given and the boats shoved off; one pinnace, commanded by Mr. Caulfield, the first lieutenant, pulling for the polacre ship, while the others went to take possession of the brigs and zebecque.

" To our astonishment, as soon as the pinnace was alongside the ship, she was received with a murderous fire, and half of our boat's crew were laid beneath the thwarts ; the remainder boarded. Caulfield was the first on the vessel's decks—a volley of musquetoons received him, and he fell dead with thirteen bullets in his body. But he was amply avenged ; out of the whole crew of the privateer, but fifteen, who escaped below and hid themselves, remained alive ; no quarter was shown, they were cut to atoms on the deck, and those who threw themselves into the sea to save their lives were shot as they struggled in the water. The fire of the privateer had been the signal for the batteries to open, and now was presented the animated scene of the boats boarding in every direction, with more or less resistance ; the whole bay reverberating with the roar of cannon, the smooth water ploughed up in every quarter by the shot directed against the frigate and boats, while the *Impérieuse* returned the fire, warping round and round with her springs to silence the most galling. This continued for nearly an hour, by which time the captured vessels were under all sail, and then the *Impérieuse* hove up her anchor, and, with the English colours waving at her gaff, and still keeping up an undiminished fire, sailed slowly out the victor."

It was on such an occasion as this, if not in this very affair, that Marryat is said to have had the adventure recorded by him in "Frank Mildmay." Like the hero of that story, he was knocked down by the body of his leader, who was shot in front of him in a boarding affair, and then almost trampled to death by the men who pressed on to carry the prize. When the fight was over he was dragged out insensible, and laid among the dead. The unfriendly remark of a comrade — that he had cheated the gallows—revived him to give a vigorous denial. Mrs. Ross Church states that this happened in Arcassan Bay during the first cruise of the *Impérieuse*, but Cochrane himself mentions no such fight there, and no loss of any of his officers. Frank Mildmay's adventure happened in Arcassan Bay, but Marryat would have obvious reasons for not being strictly accurate as to place. If the incident was taken from his own life, it can only have happened at Almeria. It may be noted that both Mr. Handstone in the novel, and Mr. Caulfield in history, were first lieutenants, and that both died in the same way, riddled with bullets, at the head of a boarding party. Was Caulfield oppressed with a presentiment of his coming death like the lieutenant in "Frank Mildmay"—or was he indeed the original of that officer who, be it observed, is a very distinct character, and has much the air of being a portrait? Perhaps a preliminary question ought to be asked, namely, whether this incident did actually happen to Marryat as recorded in the novel? It is possible. The fact that he does not mention it in the passage quoted above proves nothing. It is apparently taken from his unfinished life of his friend Napier, in which he would naturally not dwell on his own personal adventures. On the other hand, it is very much the sort of story which might be transferred from the hero of the novel to its author.

In the course of 1808 a great change came over the war in the Western Mediterranean. Napoleon made his famous (and infamous) grab at the Spanish monarchy, and instantly, without hesitation, without concert among themselves, in one great spontaneous burst of patriotic enthusiasm, the Spanish people rose in arms. Their efforts were often unsuccessful, and even disgraced by mismanagement or treason; but, on the whole, they set Europe a magnificent example, which was well followed later on by Russia, and they gave England what she had long wished for in vain—a field of battle on land against Napoleon. The *Impérieuse* had her share in the Peninsular War. It was her duty not only to help the Spaniards in the coast towns, but to harass the French troops which endeavoured to enter Spain by the coast road. Cochrane was at his best in work of this kind. For months he was engaged in incessant boat attacks on the French transports, which endeavoured to reach Barcelona (then and throughout the war in their possession), by hugging the shore. With this service were mingled landing expeditions to blow up French telegraph stations or batteries, or to help the Spaniards to defend forts which commanded the road, and which the French for that very reason were particularly anxious to capture. It was Cochrane's belief to the end of his life that if he had been supplied with a flotilla of light vessels and a regiment of troops, he would have made it impossible for the French to enter Spain by the Eastern Pyrenees at all. How far he was justified in this opinion, he never was able to show. Indeed, when he was offered just such a command on condition that he would abstain from attacking Admiral Gambier in the House of Commons, he refused it. Even as it was, however, he did much. His untiring vigilance made it impossible for the French to use the sea for the transport of men or provisions, and difficult for them to use the coast route which at many places was liable to be swept by the cannon of the English frigate. They were driven to use the inland route through a poor and rugged country swarming with guerrilleros. It is known that all this part of the war proved enormously costly to the French, and much of the credit due for imposing the loss upon them must go to the *Impérieuse.* Marryat had his share of it all, and in "Frank Mildmay" he has given a carefully finished sketch of one of the sharpest pieces of service in it— the defence of Rosas, where he himself received a bayonet wound.

The desire to be back in his place in Parliament, in order that he might expose the malpractices of the

Maltese Admiralty Court (this is the motive assigned by himself, and was doubtless that of which he was most conscious), induced Cochrane to apply for leave to bring the *Impérieuse* home to England. It was granted with a facility which throws some doubt on his theory that the Admiralty feared his presence; and early in March, 1809, he dropped anchor in Plymouth Sound. Unhappily for himself, Cochrane was selected for a special piece of service before he could resume his Parliamentary work. In February of this year a French squadron had slipped out of Brest, with orders to drive off the British seventy-fours which were then watching L'Orient, to pick up three more ships at anchor there under Commodore Troude, and then to proceed to the West Indies to relieve Martinique. Admiral Willaumez, the French commander, did not escape the vigilance of the Channel squadron. His fleet was sighted at sea, followed till it entered the Pertuis d'Antioche, between the islands of Ré and Oléron, and very soon a blockading force collected under Admiral Gambier. The outcries of the London and Liverpool merchants roused the Admiralty to make great exertions for the destruction of an armament which was designed to operate in the West Indies, and would, by its mere presence in those waters, have greatly disturbed English trade. In an evil hour for Cochrane, my Lords remembered that he was well acquainted with this part of the French coast, and they resolved to send him to execute an attack on the enemy's ships. Very reluctantly, for he knew how ill he was likely to be received by officers whom he would practically supersede, he undertook the work. He

prepared a flotilla of explosion vessels and fire-ships.
In April the *Impérieuse* had joined Gambier's squadron.
A detailed account of the action which followed would
be out of place here.   Its rather melancholy history is
to be read in Cochrane's " Autobiography," and the
Minutes of the court martial on Lord Gambier.   The
squadron was in an indifferent moral condition, divided
by sour professional factions, and impatient of its
Admiral, a brave but weak officer, chiefly known as
what was called in the navy a "blue light," that is a
pious man of a somewhat Methodistical turn.   Very little
zeal was shown in supporting Cochrane.   The attack
was made on the night of April 11th, and whatever
the *Impérieuse* could do was magnificently done.   The
French fleet of eight line-of-battle ships, and some
smaller vessels, had withdrawn to the Basque Roads, at
the mouth of the Charente, and had fortified itself with
a heavy boom.   Towards that boom the English explosion and fire-ships were driven by wind and tide
after dark on the 11th.   It is doubtful whether more
than one of them reached it—but that one was commanded by Cochrane himself.   She was brought up to
the boom at half a cable's length off the French
frigate *Indienne*, and there exploded, scattering the
boom all over the mouth of the Charente.   Through
the opening thus made a few English vessels passed.
They were a mere handful, and might have been sunk
by the fire of the French, but our enemies were panic
stricken.   They cut their cables, and ran ashore.   When
day broke the French ships were fast aground, and might
every one have been destroyed ; but Lord Gambier was

an officer of the stamp peculiarly hateful to Nelson. He was prompt to conclude that enough had been done, and was loth to risk ships and men in what he thought an unnecessary way. In vain did Cochrane, who had now returned to the *Impérieuse*, hoist signal after signal urging the Admiral to attack. He told him that the enemy were ashore, and could be destroyed; that they would get off if they were not stopped; that they were actually preparing to get off. It skilled not, and Gambier remained stolidly at anchor miles off. At last Cochrane, who by this time was nearly rabid with rage, work, and want of sleep, flew into a Berserker fury. He deliberately drifted the *Impérieuse* stern first under the guns of the French liners, and then signalled that he was overpowered and in need of assistance. This desperate measure, worthy of Nelson in his most splendid moments, did at last force Admiral Gambier's hand. Some vessels were sent—when it was well-nigh too late to do any service at all—and distinctly too late to do all that ought to have been done. Three of the French liners were destroyed, but the others by throwing their guns overboard and starting their water, were able to grovel over the mud-bar of the Charente, and escape into a pool out of reach up the river. They never appeared in the West Indies certainly, but the work was half done. Cochrane went back to England— with all that was best and worst in him fermenting with fury—to make his unhappy motion of opposition in the House to the vote of thanks to Admiral Gambier. From thence came his final quarrel with the Admiralty, and the court martial on Lord Gambier, in which it is only too probable that English officers and officials of rank winked at the suppression of evidence, and something not unlike forgery. Cochrane's service in our navy was over for long years.

With this scene of mingled heroism and stupidity, the more brilliant part of Marryat's naval life came to an end. He was engaged in the Basque Roads on one of the fire-ships, and when they proved of little use, was probably recalled to the *Impérieuse.* It is to be hoped at least that he was on her deck when her captain, in an exaltation of fury, drifted her among the French liners. In point of time, however, his service was merely beginning, and he was to do good work yet, both as a subordinate and as commander; but it wanted the heroic touch of the first three years. When Cochrane was superseded from the *Impérieuse*, Marryat remained with the new captain, and under him took part in the wholly wretched Walcheren business, out of which he got—in common with some thousands of others—all that it had to give—a distinct idea of how a combined expedition ought *not* to be conducted,—and an attack of marsh fever.

From this time until the close of the Great War, he was on such active service as the overpowering supremacy we had attained at sea left to be performed. From the Scheldt he returned invalided on board the *Victorious*, 74. As soon as he was fit for service, he was appointed to the *Centaur*, 74, the flag-ship of Sir Samuel Hood, with whom he went back to the Mediterranean, but not to the stirring life of his old frigate. After a year of the seventy-four he returned home, and was appointed to the

Æolus frigate on the American station. He went out as a passenger on the *Atlas*, 64, and joined his ship at Halifax. In the *Æolus*, and then in another frigate, the *Spartan*, he became familiar with the West Indies, which are, with the Mediterranean, the scenes of so large a part of his stories. In 1812 he had served his time as midshipman, and returned home to pass. His influence was good, as the fact that he served so much in frigates proves, and he received his lieutenant's commission immediately after going through his examination (December 26, 1812). Six months later he was appointed to *L'Espiègle* sloop, and cruised in her on the north coast of South America, till he was invalided by the breaking of a blood-vessel, and sent home as a passenger on board his old frigate, the *Spartan*, which had now finished her commission. This accident, due in part to a constitutional infirmity, which ultimately proved fatal to him, occurred at Barbadoes, at a dance —perhaps a dignity ball. In 1814 he was back on the coast of America in the *Newcastle*, 58, and was again invalided home, this time from Madeira. In June, 1815, just as the Great War was closing, Marryat was promoted commander, and the first period of his life came to an end.

The years from 1809 to 1815 may be rapidly passed over, for though they added to his experience, they were colourless as compared with the cruises of the *Impérieuse*. He saw some service in them, but it was either tame, or a mere repetition of what he had seen before. The so-called "war of 1812" was in progress during part of his service in the *Spartan* and all his service in the *New-*

castle, but he saw little of it. Some boat work—and sharp work too—he went through in Boston Bay, but he saw nothing of those unlucky frigate actions with the Americans, which gave us such a disagreeable shock, and it was not his good fortune to be one of the crew of the famous *Shannon*. The capture of a small privateer or two, by so powerful a vessel as the *Newcastle*, was no important experience to a man who had seen the boarding of the *King George*, the defence of the Trinidad fort at Rosas, and the affair in the Basque Roads. An acquaintance he made with an American prisoner of war while on board the *Newcastle* was useful to him afterwards, but at the time he probably thought little about it.

His captains in these years doubtless served him as models when he began his work as a novelist, but they were none of them men of the commanding kind. The best remembered of them was Captain E. P. Brenton of the *Spartan*, brother of the famous Sir Jahleel who fought a brilliant frigate action off Naples, under the very eyes of Murat. Captain Brenton had himself done good work, but his chief reputation was made in later days, as the author of a life of St. Vincent, and a history of the Great War, which is itself mainly remembered as the object of incessant corrections, often pettifogging, commonly superfluous, and always intensely wearisome, in James's " Naval History."

Even in the most peaceful times, opportunities of facing danger come in every seaman's way. He may have his chance to save life, and he must help to fight the storm. In both of these ways Marryat distinguished himself. Few men have more frequently risked their own lives to save others. As a midshipman in the *Impérieuse* he went overboard to save a fellow midshipman. He saved the life of a seaman while serving on the *Æolus*, and narrowly escaped drowning on a similar occasion when serving in *L'Espiègle*. On this occasion he was a mile and a half off before the sloop could be brought to, and when a boat picked him up he was nearly senseless. This also was a part of experience to Marryat, for it was while overboard from *L'Espiègle* that he discovered that drowning is not an unpleasant death. It is recorded in his Life by his daughter that, first and last, "during the time he served in the navy, he was presented with twenty-seven certificates, recommendations, and votes of thanks, for saving the lives of others at the risk of his own, beside receiving a gold medal from the Humane Society." This mark of distinction given in 1818 was assuredly well deserved.

Not less pleasing to Marryat than the memory of his efforts to save others, must have been his recollection of the honour he gained in volunteering during a gale to cut away the main-yard of the *Æolus*. The story appears, more or less coloured and adapted, with so many other of his reminiscences in "Frank Mildmay." In the sober pages of Marshall, it is, however, a quite sufficiently gallant story. "On the 30th of September, 1811, in lat. 40° 50' N., long. 65° W. (off the coast of New England), a gale of wind commenced at S.E., and soon blew with tremendous fury; the *Æolus* was laid on her beam ends, her top-masts and mizen-masts were literally blown away, and she continued in this extremely perilous situation for at least half an hour. Directions were given to cut away the main-yard, in order to save the main-mast and right the ship, but so great was the danger attending such an operation considered, that not a man could be induced to attempt it until Mr. Marryat led the way. His courageous conduct in this emergency excited general admiration, and was highly approved by Lord James Townshend, one of whose ship's company he also saved by jumping overboard at sea."

Up then to the age of three-and-twenty Marryat had prepared himself to write sea stories by making his life a sea story. He had, in fact, fulfiled the counsel of perfection given to the epic poet. He had seen no great battle; the last of them had been fought before he entered the service; he had not even shared in a single ship action. But what he did not witness himself he saw through the eyes of messmates. The battles, to judge from the little said of them in his stories, do not appear to have greatly interested Marryat—perhaps he found a difficulty in realizing what one would be like, perhaps he found them unmanageable. With the single ship actions he had no such difficulty. He could tell precisely what must happen, and he had no doubt heard tales of many such pieces of fighting. Indeed, in the actual sea-life of the time, the great battles did not play a much more considerable part than they do in the novels. Of the 2,437 lieutenants on the navy list when Marryat entered the service, the very great majority had never seen a general engagement. It was thought a rather exceptional thing that Collingwood should have been present in three battles. Nelson himself only took part in four, or five, if Admiral Hotham's feeble action in the Gulf of Lyons is to be allowed the name. But most officers had seen service of some kind, and had tales to tell. Marryat, too, had been fortunate in an eminent degree. He had been wounded, but not severely—he had never been taken prisoner or shipwrecked. His service had been varied. Between 1806 and 1815 he had seen the North Sea, the Channel, the Mediterranean, and the Eastern Coast of America, from Nova Scotia to Surinam. His promotion had been rapid. Altogether he had had much to develop, and nothing to sour him, in this first period of his life.

CHAPTER IV.

WHEN the great war came at last to an end in 1815, leaving Marryat a commander at the age of three-and-twenty, his ambition was still to be the successful naval officer, and not the portrait painter of the sea life. Twelve years were to pass before he ceased to be employed. During this period he held three commands, and once more saw the face of war. It was a small and poor war after the heroic conflicts of his boyhood, but still it had its own difficulties and trials. He began to use his pen in these years, but at first it was for merely professional purposes. His code of signals must have been prepared, and his pamphlet on the best method of recruiting the navy, and his scheme for stopping Channel smuggling, were certainly written, in this second period, while he was still looking forward to the chance of hoisting his flag.

Marryat was one of the great swarm of Englishmen who profited by the peace to visit the Continent, which had been as nearly as might be shut to the peaceful traveller for twenty-two years. He is credited with having "occupied himself in acquiring a perfect knowledge of such branches of science as might prove useful should the Lords of the Admiralty think fit to employ him in a voyage of discovery or survey." Doubtless Marryat loved his profession, and worked at it, but when he was recalled from Italy, in 1818, on some vague scheme of African exploration he was probably engaged in amusing himself. The scheme came to nothing, and in January, 1819, he married —a most convincing proof that his intention of exploring Africa had not lasted long. Mrs. Marryat was a Miss Shairp, daughter of a Scotch gentleman who had been Consul-General in Russia. Marryat never agreed with St. Vincent that married men are ruined for the service, and some eighteen months later he was at sea again in command of the *Beaver* sloop.

In this commission he saw the end of the man who had kept Europe in turmoil for the major part of a generation. The *Beaver* was ordered on an all-round cruise in the South Atlantic to show the flag at Madeira and the Azores, at the solitary rock of Tristan d'Acunha, at our own possessions at the Cape, and finally to do guard duty at St. Helena. When the *Beaver* arrived at her station Napoleon was just reaching the end of his final years of imprisonment. We still maintained a naval guard against the enterprises of any Buonapartist adventurer who might try to take the Emperor off the rock where he sat, consumed with unavailing regrets, and disgracing his fall by undignified squabbles with Sir Hudson Lowe. An English man-of-war was always kept cruising to windward of the island. The last officer who performed this duty was Captain Marryat. The *Beaver* was watching for the possible liberator, who never came, when Napoleon died. Marryat, who was a clever draughtsman, took a sketch of the Emperor on his death-bed. He was already apparently suffering from dysentery or he fell ill immediately (and somewhat conveniently) afterwards. As his health did not permit him to remain in the South Atlantic station any longer, he was allowed to exchange into the *Rosario*. In her he brought the despatches announcing the Emperor's death home to Spithead. From Spithead he was ordered round to Harwich to form part of the squadron which escorted the body of Queen Caroline to Cuxhaven. This piece of ceremonial duty was followed by work of a very different kind. The *Rosario* was told off for revenue duty in the Channel, and continued cruising for smugglers till she was put out of commission in February, 1822. This was service of a very sufficiently serious kind. There was indeed no fighting to be done, but the cruising was arduous and incessant. The smugglers were among the smartest seamen in the Channel, and to catch them required on the part of the revenue officers constant vigilance, great activity, and an intimate knowledge of the coast—that is to say, if the work was to be properly done. As a matter of fact it seems to have been scamped. Marryat, who had perhaps been infected by Cochrane with an inability to let a comfortable old abuse alone, forwarded to the Admiralty a long despatch showing that the preventive service was inefficiently performed, and pointing out how it could be improved. The despatch was written after the *Rosario* had been paid off, and was founded on his own experience. It gives a curious glimpse into a phase of sea life which has entirely disappeared since the establishment of free trade ruined the smugglers by making it not worth any man's while to smuggle. The industry which went on all round the coast, from the mouth of the Clyde to the mouth of the Firth of Forth, was conducted on varying principles in different districts. Marryat dealt only with what he had seen himself:—the smuggling carried on in that part of the English Channel which lies between Portsmouth and the Start.

When he came to write as a novelist, Marryat displayed a certain sympathy with the adventurous scamps who ran cargoes of brandy from Cherbourg to the coast of Hampshire and Dorsetshire. But Captain Marryat the revenue officer was a very different person. In this severe and official capacity he did his best to suppress what he afterwards described with a distinctly humorous sympathy. The smugglers, he pointed out, profited by the system adopted by the English revenue boats. Cherbourg was the centre of the trade—the free trade, as the smugglers called it, not knowing, poor fellows, who their real enemy was. Their vessels were almost exclusively manned by Portland or Weymouth men. When they were going to run a cargo to a point of the coast with which they were not familiar, they would take on a local hand, but as a rule they kept the trade pretty exclusively to themselves. When one of their luggers was sighted by the revenue boats and could not show a clean pair of heels, the cargo was jettisoned. If this happened in mid-channel it was a clear loss to everybody. The smuggler crews were only paid when they landed a cargo. The revenue boats could get no prize money unless they seized the tubs of spirits. If, however, the cargo was jettisoned in shallow water, the case was different. The smugglers might return, or their confede-rates on shore could fish up the sunken kegs, and then of course they earned their money. On the other hand, if the landing was stopped, or the kegs were dredged up by the revenue officers *they* earned their prize money. It is therefore perfectly obvious that it was the interest of the revenue officers not to see the smuggling luggers in mid-channel. The more brandy they picked up, the more prize money they earned, and the more credit also. But by allowing the smugglers to approach the English coast they gave them many opportunities of running cargoes. Partly because they wished to secure the approval of their chiefs, who took no account of any service which did not include the capture of kegs— partly also out of a natural human desire for prize money, the revenue boats nursed the illicit trade. They went very little to sea, and confined their exertions to scouring the coasts in cutters and gigs. Marryat's idea was that much more effect would be produced by pursuing the luggers in mid-channel. If, he argued with great force, the smugglers found that they were com-pelled to make a dead loss, voyage after voyage, they would soon become tired. As it was, the immense profits earned on any cargo successfully run, paid them for the loss of two, or even three. Of course if his system were adopted there would be no captures to show for the credit of the coastguard, and no prize money to be earned. But the smuggling would be put a stop to. The despatch in which he set forth his opinions is a thoroughly able and business-like document, and shows that if Marryat was allowed to fall out of the service it was not because he was wanting in zeal or ability.

Although Marryat, like every other naval officer who ever held His Majesty's commission, thought himself "no favourite" with the Admiralty, he had no intelligible reason to complain—at least as yet. The grumblings of naval officers are generally, indeed, unintelligible to the landsman, who is apt, after hearing much of them, to arrive at the conclusion that if every gentleman in the service were promoted to be Lord High Admiral and made G.C.B. to morrow morning, they would all be as discontented as ever by midday. Certainly Marryat, who was a commander at twenty-three, and had received a command, on service which brought him into notice, in time of profound peace and reduction of armaments, when the great majority of his fellow officers were vegetating on half pay on shore, had little cause to growl. He must, in truth, have had very good influence at the Admiralty, for though he was only paid off the *Rosario* in February, 1822, he was re-appointed to the *Larne*, of twenty guns, in March, 1823, so that he had barely a year on shore. The *Larne* was fitted out at Portsmouth for service in the East Indies. In July Marryat sailed from Spithead for his station, this time taking out his wife and family. An entry in his log briefly records an accident which might, if the amplified form of the story given in his biography is to be taken as literally true, have ended his career in a somewhat absurd manner. His gig upset in Falmouth Harbour while he was in it. To an athletic man and good

swimmer a ducking in the month of July was no great
disaster, but the boat carried a bumboat woman and a
midshipman. The woman swam like a fish, and was
delighted at the prospect of distinction and profit
apparently thrown in her way. She fastened on Marryat,
intent on saving a captain, and refused peremptorily to
let him go when she was asked to transfer her help from
the superior officer, who did not need it, to the obscure
midshipman, who, not being able to swim, was in
imminent danger of drowning. In some way or another
Marryat did contrive to get rid of the incumbrance of
her assistance, and the mid was not sacrificed. Whether
he did not invent the bumboat woman's devotion to rank,
is perhaps doubtful. A bumboat woman was capable of
acting in this way, no doubt, but then Marryat was
equally capable of seeing that she ought to behave in
this way, and of crediting her with fulfilling her duty.

When the *Larne* reached India, Marryat found that
she was to form part of the combined force ordered to
invade Burmah. This war, which filled 1824 and 1825,
was of a kind common with us before we learnt that in
war, as in building, it is more economical to employ a
hundred men for one day, than one man for a hundred
days—before also the common use of steam had made
great rapidity of movement possible. Sir Archibald
Campbell's force was not numerous enough, and was
unable to move quick. The operations dragged on for
months, till fevers, cholera, and scurvy, had almost
annihilated our army, and had almost unmanned the
squadron. The duties of the navy, in the war, were to
clear the Irrawaddy of Burmese war-boats, to transport

the troops, protect their landing, cover their flank, and
now and then to help storm a stockade, or beat down the
fire of native batteries mounted with guns which would
not fire, handled by gunners who could not shoot. The
enemy fought fiercely, according to his lights, but then he
had neither good weapons, nor discipline, nor experience.
Except when attacked in a particularly strong position,
by an insufficient force, the poor Burmese were sent into
action as cattle to the slaughter. We naturally make the
most of these wars, and politically they are often of the
utmost importance, but as far as fighting is concerned, a
wilderness of them is not equal to the action between
the *Shannon* and the *Chesapeak*, or the *Blanche* and the
Pique. Yet Marryat was well entitled to say, as he did
in a letter to his brother Samuel, that the crew of the
Larne had in the course of five months " undergone a
severity of service almost unequalled." The climate
was deadly to unseasoned men exposed to it in an
unhealthy season. Much toil had to be gone through
in moving the troops, in rowing guard against the
Burmese war-boats, and even in doing engineer work.
It is a complaint sometimes made by the navy that,
in combined operations with the army, a dispropor-
tionate amount of the toil falls to them, while the
redcoats get all the fun and the glory of the fighting.
In this war the navy had plenty of work, and suffered
proportionately from the strain. It also complained, in
later days, that its exertions were hardly sufficiently
recognized by military historians. Yet their compara-
tively subordinate position was a necessity of the case.
The war was a land, and not a naval war, and the

sailors could hardly expect to be more than accessories in it.

Marryat's share, both of the work and the credit, was as large as that of any naval officer engaged. From the beginning of the campaign, in May, 1824, he was employed until September; at first as subordinate, and then, when Commodore Grant was invalided, as senior naval officer at Rangoon. The five months almost destroyed the crew of the *Larne*, and greatly damaged his own health. His men had been on salt provisions since February, and when fatigue and exposure were added to unwholesome diet, they naturally suffered grievously from scurvy. After a rest at Pulo Penang, he was back at Rangoon in December, and then, after being despatched on service to India, he was recalled to Burmah to take part in an attack on Bassein. There were more river work, more attacks on stockades, more exposure to fever. In July, 1824, on the death of Commodore Grant, he was transferred into the *Tees*, 26, a post-ship, which—as it was a death vacancy—should have given him post rank. The nomination was not, however, confirmed by the Admiralty, and Marryat was not actually posted till 1825, a loss of a year, which affected his seniority. It was in the *Larne* that he took part in the occupation of Bassein, and the attack on the Burmese stockades at Negrais and Naputah, but he brought the *Tees* home and paid her off early in 1826. The thanks of the general and the Indian Government, the Companionship of the Bath, and the command of the *Ariadne*, 28, were his rewards for good service in Burmah. This command he held for exactly two years, from November, 1828, to November, 1830, when "private affairs" induced him to resign. The *Ariadne* was his last ship. He was never employed again, nor does he ever seem to have applied for a command. When there was a prospect of war with the United States some years later, he spoke of going on active service again, but he was in ordinary times quite reconciled apparently to the termination of his career as a naval officer. The end was rather sudden. Up to 1830 he had been in constant employment and very successful. He could hardly have hoped for more than to be a post-captain and a C.B. at thirty-four. The truth doubtless is that he had begun to have other ambitions.

As is not uncommonly the case, the end of the old life overlapped the beginning of the new. Indeed, the old cannot have consciously come to an end with Marryat for some years. The evidence as to his wishes and hopes is scanty—extraordinarily scanty considering his prominence and that he lived almost into this generation; but what has been made known about him shows that he did not cease to think and work for "the service," or quite gave up for a long time expecting that he might again hold a command. As an active naval officer, however, his career ended when he resigned the command of the *Ariadne*. Before that date he had written and published "Frank Mildmay," and had written the "King's Own." What the private affairs may have been which induced him to resign his ship does not appear very clearly. Mrs. Ross Church supposes that he wished to devote himself to his duties as equerry to the Duke of Sussex, which hardly appears a sufficient explanation.

Perhaps, like many other sailors, he may have had a
period of revolt against the routine work, and long
absence from friends and family imposed by naval life,
and for which there is little compensation in peace time.
With a growing family to look after he had a strong attrac-
tion to the shore. Then service in peace time cannot
have had many temptations to a man who enjoyed excitement as Marryat did. To be sent on " diplomatic duties,"
which in practice would mean visits, in the company of His
Majesty's Consuls, to foreign governors, or to be ordered
off in winter to look for reefs in the Atlantic, which never
existed except in the bemused brains of some merchant
skipper, must have been very trying. An experience or
two of this kind, coinciding with the success of his first
book and the equerryship, would be enough to decide
him to try his fortune on shore—all the more as he had
private means. Whatever the exact motives may have
been, in 1830 he was on shore for good, and established
in Sussex House, Hammersmith.

His equerryship seems to have led him to no particular good. "The smiles of princes," says Mrs. Church,
"are by nature evanescent." The favour of princes at
least, like that of other men, requires to be cultivated
with due skill and attention. Possibly Marryat may
have been wanting in the will or the capacity to practise
the art. Certain it is that neither from the Duke of
Sussex, nor from the duke's royal brother, William IV.,
did he ever obtain any visible good beyond invitations
to festivities which appear to have been of a somewhat
dreary character. According to a story given in the
preface to Bone's edition of the " Pirate and Three

Cutters," and quoted on that authority by Mrs. Ross
Church, the King, who all through his life seems to have
been moved to do something silly whenever he remembered that he was a naval officer, was offended by
Marryat's condemnation of the pressgang. He not only
refused to consent to the conferring of some mark of distinction on Marryat in addition to the C.B. given for the
Burmah campaign, but would not even allow him to wear
the Legion of Honour sent him by Louis Philippe as a
reward for the code of signals. The story is credible
enough of William IV., who, saving the reverence of
the Crown, was very little better than a fool, and a
spiteful fool, too, at times. The Admiralty of its own
motion, or the Admiralty and the King together, seem
to have decided that Marryat need not be employed
again. In the enjoyment of literary success and liberty,
he probably reconciled himself to the want of employment readily enough. He must have been prepared to
do without it when he threw up his command. The
Admiralty does not love captains who resign their ships.

CHAPTER V.

FROM 1830 to his death in 1848 Marryat was a working man of letters, and a busy one. His books were many, and they do not represent all his labours. There was a life of his old messmate, Lord Napier, begun—and stopped—at the request of the widow, and much miscellaneous journalism—if tha is the correct description of contributions to magazines. His pen was rapid, and he had no fear of tackling new subjects, so that the length of the shelf which would hold his complete works would be considerable, and the variety of the contents of the edition not small. Sea stories and land stories, plays which never reached the stage, diaries on the Continent and in America, letters of Norfolk farmers, and didactic tales for children all went in.

There is a difficulty in the way of the telling of Marryat's own life during these busy eighteen years—the not uncommon difficulty, want of information. The biography published by his family leaves much unexplained, for reasons into which it would be useless, even if one had the right, to inquire. The causes of Marryat's sudden changes of residence, and of his hasty journey to

the Continent in 1835, are only to be guessed at. He
did not live much in the literary world of his time. Of
the eighteen years of his writing activity, several in the
middle were spent on the Continent, and several at the
end in Norfolk. In a general way one gathers that the
question of money was a very important, sometimes a
very pressing one, with Marryat. Money earned, inherited, spent—money to be recovered from debtors,
and, doubtless, paid to creditors, had much of his attention. It is manifest that he was what Carlyle would
· have called "a very expensive Herr." He liked to lead
a large life, and to show a gentlemanly indifference to
money. By preference he lived in good houses, in good
neighbourhoods, and it is not overrash or uncharitable
to guess that his income was not always adequate to his
expenses. Finally, he was addicted to some of the most
effectual of all methods of evacuation. If he did not
promote, or have to face, a petition, at least he went
through a contested election; and he had Balzac's
mania for ingenious speculations, which ought to have
realized wealth beyond the dreams of avarice, and did
achieve a dead loss with the most unfailing regularity.
Like many another sailor before and since, he was sure
that he could show the trained farmer how to extract
more than he had yet done from the land. He undertook
to do so on his small estate at Langham, in Norfolk—
with disastrous financial results. That farming speculation was undoubtedly the type of much in his life.

His movements, if not the causes of them, can be
followed easily enough. Between 1830 and his departure for America in 1837, he was successively at Sussex

House, Hammersmith ; at Langham, in Norfolk ; then back in London ; then in Brighton ; then in sudden haste off to Brussels ; and from thence to Lausanne. " Frank Mildmay ; or, The Naval Officer," appeared in 1829. Nine months later, when he was fixed on shore, came out the " King's Own." In 1830 he acquired a thousand acres of land in Norfolk, which remained in his possession till his death. He exchanged Sussex House for it, but how Sussex House was got we are not told. It cannot have been bought either out of prize money, or the proceeds of the two books he had published already, although his prices were remarkably good for a beginner. Four hundred pounds is the sum said to have been given by Colburn for " Frank Mildmay "—a good deal more than the most sanguine of novices would expect to receive from the most generous of publishers for a first book in these days. Certainly, in 1830, Marryat was working as a man works who has reasons for making all the money he can. He was contributing to the *Metropolitan Magazine*, and receiving his sixteen pounds a sheet—which, again, is good magazine pay. It did not take him long to acquire a shrewd idea how to deal with publishers, and a distinct understanding of the due privileges of an editor. His knowledge of these important matters is shown conclusively in a letter to Bentley, setting forth the terms on which he would be prepared to edit a new nautical magazine, a proposed imitation of, or rather rival to, the *United Service Journal.*

" My terms," he says, with the confidence of a man who knew the market, and his own value in it, " would be as follows : The sole control of the work, for when I do my best I must be despotic or I shall not succeed; to be paid for all my writings at the price I received in the *Metropolitan*, sixteen guineas per sheet. The editorship I would then take at £400 per annum until the end of the first year, when, if the work succeeded, I should expect an addition of £100, and if it continued profitable, another £100, so as to raise the *final* pay of the editor to £600 per annum. The stipulations may be talked over afterwards. To choose my sub-editor is indispensable. He must be a nautical man." Marryat had learnt plainly how necessary it is to be captain of your own ship—and withal he quite understood how to launch the new kind of craft he was about to sail. "The first number must be most carefully got up, to insure success, and the papers ought now to be in preparation. You must, therefore, take but few days to decide, as I tell you honestly I have reason to expect the offer from another quarter, who are now talking the matter over, and I must be allowed to consider myself as unpledged to you after a short time."

As it is not recorded that Marryat had, like Arthur Pendennis, any George Warrington to guide his literary beginnings, he deserves all the more credit for his spontaneous appreciation of the advantage to be obtained by playing Bacon off against Bungay.

"The offer from another quarter," which was thus quoted to hasten the decision of Mr. Bentley, was the editorship of the *Metropolitan*, which he took in 1832, and held until he left England for Brussels. He either received as part payment, or purchased a proprietary right in the magazine, which he afterwards sold to Saunders

and Otley for £1,050. For the next four or five years
the *Metropolitan* had the major part of Marryat's time
and work. He had, according to his wish, a nautical
sub-editor, the E. Howard, who wrote that strange book,
"Rattlin the Reefer," which still continues to be catalogued
with Marryat's own stories. There were contributors to be
hunted up—kept up to the mark, more or less successfully
—and occasionally soothed down—Thomas Moore for
one, who wrote in agony to insist on the necessity there was
that he should see his proofs, and also to make monetary
arrangements. Of course there were quarrels to be
fought out, for in those days no periodical was able to
exist without its regular battle. But in the midst of
these forgetable and forgotten things—Marryat contributed to the *Metropolitan* five of the best of his
books. "Newton Forster" appeared in 1832, "Peter
Simple" in 1833 ; and in 1834 no less than three—"Jacob
Faithful," "Mr. Midshipman Easy," and "Japhet in
Search of a Father." Not a little of what, to apply nautical language, may be called dunnage appeared with and
after these—a comedy, a tragedy (of neither of which
does Marryat seem to have thought highly), and a host
of miscellaneous papers collected under the title of
"Olla Podrida"—these last being only what Marryat
frankly called his "Diary on the Continent"—namely,
"very good magazine stuff."

His extraordinary industry in 1834 can be confidently
accounted for by the need of money. In 1833 he had
taken effectual means to lighten his purse by standing for
Parliament. The constituency chosen for the venture
was the Tower Hamlets, and Marryat stood as a

Reformer. Although the year immediately following the passing of the Reform Bill was as good a one as he could well have found in which to try in that character, he was not successful. His reforming zeal was possibly too purely naval for the constituency, and he was wanting in the very necessary readiness to say ditto to a popular fad. Marryat seems to have considered that his dislike of the press-gang was claim enough to the character of Liberal Reformer. But in the midst of profound peace the press-gang was not a burning grievance, and on some other points he took a line not likely to prove pleasing to the sentimental among the Liberals, for whose votes he was asking. He could not be got to show a burning interest in the sorrows of the slave. He took up the logically strong, but practically ineffective, position of the man who declined to be troubled for the slave while there was so much suffering unremedied at home. This might be a very sensible decision, but unfortunately it was discredited by the fact that it had been a favourite one with the slave-holders, whose tenderness for sufferers at home was never heard of till their own property in the West Indies seemed to be in danger. On another question, which proved a trying one to candidates till very recently, Marryat took a disastrously sensible course. He was called upon to give his opinion of the practice of flogging in the navy—and committed himself to the side of discipline most fatally. "Sir," he said to a heckler, who wanted to know whether the "gallant captain" would be capable of flogging him or his sons; "Sir, you say the answer I gave you is not direct; I will answer you again. If ever you, or one of your sons,

should come under my command, and deserve punishment, if there be no other effectual mode of conferring
it, I shall flog you." After that it is not surprising to
hear that "Captain Marryat and the Chairman left the
room together, amidst a tumult of united applause and
disapprobation"—in the midst, in fact, of an uproar, in
which the part of the meeting which admired his pluck
was engaged in shouting against the other part which
detested his good sense. There was something of
Colonel Newcome in the politics of Captain Marryat,
and he had not the good fortune to contend against a
Barnes Newcome. His parliamentary ambition had to
take its place with the other schemes of his life which
came to nothing. A plan for the establishment of brevet
rank in the navy, which he sent in about this time to
Sir James Graham, was part of his activity as a political
naval officer. It also came to nothing, and nobody can
well regret that it was still-born.

After the misspent energy of 1833, Marryat had to
make up by hard pen-work. He settled in Montpelier
Villas, Western Road, Brighton, and there, in 1834, wrote
his three books. The effort was a severe one, and he felt
the effects later on, when fatigue, and possibly questions of
money, had induced him to go abroad. He had not yet
altogether given up thinking of Parliament—or, at least,
if he had ceased hoping to sit as member, he kept up
his correspondence with ministers on those naval affairs
which he understood. He forwarded observations on
the Merchant Shipping Bill of that year—one of our
portentous list of shipping measures—to Sir James
Graham. His volunteer help was well received, and the

First Lord, one of the ablest men who ever was at the head of the department, invited him to come to Whitehall and talk the Bill over. This invitation may be taken as a proof, among others, that if Marryat remained unemployed, it was mainly by his own wish. He had already, by his writing on the manning of the navy, and, in less public ways, shown that in professional matters, at least, he was an excellent man of business. Sir James Graham was not the man to have refused employment to an officer of proved ability if he had wished for it, but it is tolerably plain that Marryat had other irons of a more attractive kind, for the moment, in the fire.

The particular iron which he had heating in Norfolk —the estate at Langham—was not likely to relieve him from the necessity of making every penny he could by his pen. "No rent," was his return in 1834, and as a rule ever after—till he took it in hand himself, and then it still realized him a steady yearly deficit. This year of "no rent" was also a year of legal unpleasantness in connection with his father's memory—which he bore in a fashion to be recommended to the imitation of all who suffer from similar misfortunes. "As for the Chancellor's judgment," he wrote to his mother, who had plainly been hurt, "I cannot say I thought anything about it ; on the contrary, it appears to me that he might have been much more severe if he had thought proper. It is easy to impute motives, and difficult to disprove them. I thought, considering his enmity, that he let us off cheap, as there is no *punishing a Chancellor*, and he might say what he pleased with impunity. I did not, therefore, *roar*, I only *smiled*. The effect will be nugatory. Not one in a thousand will read it; those who do, know it refers to a person not in this world, and of those, those who knew my father will not believe it; those who did not will care little about it, and forget the name in a week. Had he given the decision in our favour, I should have been better pleased, but *it's no use crying; what's done can't be helped.*" With that piece of the philosophy of the elder Faithful, Marryat ends as neat a statement of reasons for not making a fuss, and as admirable an estimate of the relative unimportance of any man's private affairs in a busy world, as will be found by much searching.

Next year Marryat was off in haste to the Continent. "Not one day was our departure postponed; with post horses and postillions, we posted, post haste, to Brussels." As is too commonly the case, Mrs. Ross Church has nothing to say as to the cause of this flight—and we are left to conclude that it was due to that desire to economize with dignity which has driven so many Englishmen to the same voluntary exile. At Brussels or at Spa he went on working for the *Metropolitan.* He cannot have edited it, but he sent in his " Diary on the Continent," and he wrote, in this year, "'The Pirate " and "The Three Cutters," in which, for the first time, he had the advantage of being illustrated by Clarkson Stanfield. With the *Metropolitan* his connection was coming to an end. In 1836 he returned to England, to get rid of his proprietary interest in it to Saunders and Otley, and to part with those publishers in a friendly manner—but to part decisively, on the ground that they would hear nothing of an advance for fresh work. *The*

New Monthly was now his resource—at the increased
rate of twenty guineas a sheet. To 1836 belong
"Snarley Yow" and "The Pasha of Many Tales,"—and
also the beginning of that "Life of Lord Napier" which
was never to be finished. In 1837 he had begun to feel
the need of a change, the desire to break fresh ground,
and in April, leaving his family at Lausanne, he started
for the United States.

His life during these two years of foreign residence
may probably be fairly well realized by the reader who
will give himself the pleasure to remember some parts of
Thackeray and many parts of Lever. The Marryats
must have formed part of that English colony on the
Continent at the head of which marched the Marquess
of Steyne, while Captain Rook and the Honourable Mr.
Deuceace brought up the rear. It was a society much
more merry than wise, and it is to be feared more easy
than honest. Its members lived abroad to escape something—perhaps it was only restraint, perhaps it was the
heavy bills of English tradesmen not yet reclaimed from
the evil ways of long credit and high prices, sometimes
it was the sheriff's-officer. Now and then it was only the
English winter. That was the most wholesome reason;
but it was the least commonly genuine, and the most
frequently assumed. In all that curious expatriated
world there was something of the Cave of Adullam. It
was often only the more pleasant on that account.
Acquaintances matured quickly; among people who
were all more or less fugitives, few questions were
asked; even Captain Rook and Mr. Deuceace were
received without too much inquiry by people who

neither imitated nor liked all their ways. Now we are
less strict at home, and by a natural reaction more
circumspect abroad. Besides railways keep people
rolling, and have greatly broken up the old English
colonies. Still even now there is a continental English
society, less Bohemian than the old, but still somewhat
free and easy, addicted as it were to living in its shirt
sleeves, very pleasant to see, and to go through, but not
at all good to be lived in for the moral man. During
the thirties this Cave of Adullam was in full swing,
crowded with refugees—not for political causes—with
veterans of the old war intent on making pension and
half-pay go as far as possible, and with pleasure-seeking
people ready for any amusement (the cheaper the better),
and not too exacting as to the moral qualities or social
position of those with whom they were prepared to
amuse themselves.

Marryat with his abundant spirits, his faculty for story-
telling, and his sufficient command of money, would
naturally fall on his feet in this rather gypsy world. He
spoke French fluently, and his wife, as the daughter of
an English consul in Russia, would be at home in
continental society. Once more it must be confessed
that the details are wanting. Mrs. Ross Church says,
that "to this hour" (she wrote in 1872) "many anec-
dotes are related of him by the older residents at
Brussels." Sadly few of them seem to have been
collected, for Mrs. Ross Church can only muster two
—neither, it must be confessed, very brilliant nor very
honourable. According to the first, Marryat was asked
to dinner to meet a company of celebrities and friends

of his own, in hopes that he would talk. He held his tongue, and when asked whether he had been silent because he was bored, answered, "Why did you imagine I was going to let out any of my jokes for those fellows to put in their next books? No, that is not *my* plan. When I find myself in such company as *that*, I open my ears and hold my tongue, glean all I can, and give them nothing in return." The story needs a good deal of explaining before the point of it becomes obvious; and unluckily the circumstances, which could alone explain it, are wanting. The fun, if there was any, was supplied (we must suppose) by the character of the person it was said to—and who was he? The other story contains a repartee—an awful repartee—a thing to be put in a collection of witticisms with the comment that "so and so smiled, but never forgave the jest." It is about the bridge of somebody's nose, and is not greatly inferior to the recorded jokes of Douglas Jerrold.

There is little to be gleaned out of such reminiscences as these, which hardly reach the dignity of "dead nettles": neither do we gather much from a surviving letter to Mr. Osmond de Beauvoir Priaulx about a debt of frs. 1250, owed to Marryat by R——, a hopeless debt. "I consider that if I have no better chance of heaven than of R——'s 1250 francs, I am in a bad way. Both he and Z—— are evidently a couple of rogues. The only chance of obtaining the money from R—— is by telling him that I am coming to Paris as soon as I can, and that I shall expose him by publishing the whole affair, his letters, &c.; and, moreover that you *strongly suspect* that it is my intention, independent of exposure, to *break*

every bone in his body on my arrival. He holds himself
as a gentleman, being the son of some post-captain, and
will not like that message, and may perhaps pay the
money rather than incur the risk." Here obviously was
a very pretty quarrel ; but who was R——, and had he a
case, and who was Mr. Osmond de Beauvoir Priaulx,
and did any assault follow? Who knows? and indeed
who cares? The rest of the letter is full of scandal
about capital letters and dashes. The sight of it only
make one remember how much entirely unimportant
trash contrives to survive in this world.

All the scraps of knowledge about Marryat which have
escaped destruction are not so unpleasant, though they
are nearly as obscure, as that letter to Mr. Osmond de
Beauvoir Priaulx. It is recorded that he gave parties and
Christmas trees, that he looked after children well, and
was a neat hand at packing a portmanteau,—qualities
which must have made him the most tolerable of
husbands and fathers on his travels. He was at all
times tender-hearted with children, as befitted an author
who ended by writing almost wholly for them ; and
would quiet his own by telling them stories, when the
rattling of carriages and diligences had made them
fractious. A letter to his mother survives from these
years which is worth quoting—not because it gives much
information about his own life, but because it is kindly, and
gives a very different picture of Marryat to that afforded
by the threats against R——, and the vapid scandal
written to the gentleman with the handsome French
name.

"SPA, *June* 9, 1835.

"MY DEAREST MOTHER,—It is dreadfully hot, and we are all gasping for breath. Kate is very unwell. She cannot walk now, and is obliged to go out in the carriage. Children thrive. As for me, I am teaching myself German, and writing a little now and then ''The Diary of a Blasé:' one part has appeared in the *Metropolitan*—very good magazine stuff. I have a fractional part of the gout in my middle right finger. Is it possible to make V—— a member of the Horticultural? He is very anxious, and he deserves it; the personal knowledge is the only difficulty; but I know him, and I am part of you, and therefore you know him. Will that syllogism do? We are as quiet here as if we were out of the world, and I like it. I wanted quiet to recover me. Since I have been here I have discovered what I fancy will be new in England—a variety of carnation, with short stalks—the stalks are so short that the flowers do not rise above the leaves of the plant, and you have no idea how pretty they are ; they are all in a bush (? blush). There are two varieties here, belonging to a man, but he will not part with them. He says they are very scarce, and only to be had at Vervier, a town eight miles off. They are celebrated for flowers at Liége, but a flower-woman from Liége, to whom I showed them, said she had never seen them there ; so I presume the man was correct. Have you heard of them? By-the-by, you should ask V—— to send for some Ghent roses—they are extremely beautiful. I did give most positive orders that Fred should not go out unless with Mr. B— or one of the masters. He remained three days in Paris, having escaped from the gentleman who had charge of him, and cannot, or will not, account for where he was, or what he did. He did not go to his school until his money was gone. He is at a dangerous age now, and must be kept close. Write me or Kate a long letter, telling us all the news. I intend to come home in October, or thereabouts; but I must arrange according to Kate's manœuvres. If she goes her time of course I must be with her, and then she will winter here, I have no doubt, as we cannot travel in winter with babies, nor indeed do I wish to; as travelling costs a great deal of money—and I have none to spare.

"God bless you, mamma. This is a famous place for your complaint, if it comes on again. The cures are miraculous. Love to Ellen. She sha'n't come German over me when we meet. I don't think I ever should have learnt it, only G—— gave himself such airs about it."

The letter is not a masterpiece, but it is good-natured and wholesome. The "Fred," who had been playing truant so enviably in Paris, was afterwards the Lieutenant Frederick Marryat who perished in the wreck of the *Avenger.*

CHAPTER VI

HIS departure for America is a convenient date at which to stop and survey Marryat's literary work. After 1837, he did some things as good as anything he had done before, and some at once unlike what he had already written, and yet excellent of their kind. "Poor Jack" and "Percival Keene" have touches of the old sea life, and flashes of fun, not inferior to his earlier writing. The "Phantom Ship" has a character of its own; the children's stories of his last years are excellent. All these are later than 1837. Still, if he had ceased to write entirely in that year, his place in literature would be as high as it is. We should have "The King's Own," "Peter Simple," "Mr. Midshipman Easy," "Japhet," "Jacob Faithful," and "Snarley Yow," and with these we should possess the best of him. In those eight busy years Marryat had poured out the harvest of his experience profusely. His beginning in literature had been singularly fortunate. The time was favourable to writers of any originality certainly. A brilliant magazine article made a reputation. There was a marked readiness to recognize ability and reward it. What amount of praise and pudding would be given in

these days for another essay on Milton it would be useless to guess, but undoubtedly it could hardly be greater
than the share which fell to Macaulay for his early effort.
Carlyle made a place for himself by a few articles. The
wind which blew for them blew for others also. As has
almost always been the case in great literary periods, the
readiness of the reader to recognize and admire was as
strong as the productive power of the writer. The
audience met the playwright half way. Sir Walter Scott
had prepared the market for the novelist. He had
enormously increased the taste for novels, and whoever
could write at all was the surer of a hearing, because
"Waverley" had made stories a necessity to readers.
There is among the more atrabilious kind of men of
letters a secret belief that the sum of popularity is a fixed
quantity, of which whatever is earned by one man is necessarily lost by another. That one nation's gain is another's
loss in commerce, was an accepted axiom with economists
of the days of darkness before Adam Smith. It has been
given up on maturer consideration, and is assuredly no
more true in literature than international trade. A great
writer who gains a great popularity increases the chance
of the smaller men. Sir Walter and Jane Austen helped
the Mrs. Meeke in whom Macaulay delighted.

Marryat had profited amply by the opening. With
great adaptability he had thrown himself into the literary
fight of his time. As has been already said, he soon
showed himself at home in the regular business of literature—in writing for the press and in editing. To take
the satisfactory though vulgar test of money, he was
able to make his market, and put his price up. Nor

was he at all reluctant to insist on the value of his goods.
"I do not," he said in 1837, "write for sixteen guineas
a sheet now.   I let them off for twenty guineas, as I do
not wish to run them hard ; and I now have commenced
with the *New Monthly* at that rate for one year certain,
and the copyright secured to me.   Times are hard, and
I do not wish to break the backs of the publishers,
although I ride over them roughshod.   I have also made
very much better terms for my books.   'Snarley Yow,'
comes out on the 1st of June.   I have parted very amicably
with Saunders and Otley, who would not stand an advance.   I *will* make hay when the sun shines ; for every
dog has his day, and I presume my time will come as
that of others."   Twenty guineas a sheet was the
exceptional price which Fraser was paying Carlyle in
those very years, and was five guineas above the usual
rate.   Obviously here was a gentleman who knew that
business was business.   With this determination to make
the last penny there was to make, he naturally contributed
his chapter to the history of the quarrels of authors with
their publishers.

"Although Captain Marryat," says his daughter, "and
his publishers mutually benefited by their transactions
with each other, one would have imagined from the
letters exchanged between them that they had been
natural enemies."   It is a mistake which is not uncommon in these transactions, and particularly likely to arise
when, as in this case, a publisher frankly tells the author
that he thinks him "eccentric," and an "odd creature,"
and adds that he is himself "somewhat warm-tempered."
Who the particular publisher was who sent these pieces

of criticism and self-criticism to Marryat we are not told. The answer he received might supply a clue to the Marryatist who was prepared to follow it up with the proper devotion.

"There was no occasion for you to make the admission that you were somewhat warm-tempered. Your letter establishes the fact. Considering your age, you are a little volcano, and if the insurance were aware of your frequent visits to the Royal Exchange, they would demand double premium for the building. Indeed, I have my surmises *now* as to the last conflagration.

* * * * * *

"Your remark as to the money I have received may sound very well, mentioned as an isolated fact; but how does it sound when it is put into juxtaposition with the sums you have received? I, who have found everything, receiving a pittance; while you, who have found nothing but the shop to sell in, receiving such a lion's share. I assert again, it is slavery. I am Sinbad the Sailor, and you are the Old Man of the Mountain (*sic*) clinging on my back, and you must not be surprised at my wishing to throw you off the first convenient opportunity.

"The fact is, you have the vice of old age very strong upon you, and you are blinded by it; but put the question to your sons, and ask them if they consider the present agreement fair. Let them arrange with me, and do you go and read your Bible. We all have our own ideas of Paradise, and if other authors think like me, the more pleasurable portion of anticipated bliss is that there will be no publishers there. That idea often supports me after an interview with one of your fraternity."

Author and publisher told one another "their fact" plainly enough in this case, and one rather wonders what lies hid under the asterisks. In the absence of information as to the proportion in which they respectively shared the profits of the stories written before 1837, one cannot undertake to say whether the unnamed publisher of fiery temper, advanced age, and small stature, received a lion's share or not. If so, it must have represented a handsome sum, for Marryat was by no means one of the worst treated of authors. Colburn gave him £400 for "Frank Mildmay." For "Mr. Midshipman Easy" he received £1,400, apparently in a lump sum. "The Pirate" and "The Three Cutters," published together, brought him in £750. His other books were paid on the same scale, and he certainly did not edit the *Metropolitan* for nothing. His code of signals, which was not literature (and perhaps on that account only the more lucrative), was an appreciable income to him throughout his life. On the whole, Marryat seems to have found the profession of author sufficiently remunerative. His indignation with his publishers may be safely taken to be mainly a proof that, in common with most writing-men of his generation, he was a firm believer in the creed that authors are an ill-used body. This is no longer quite so orthodox as it was. The wind is rather blowing the other way, and it is becoming the right thing to say that authors have themselves to thank for their ill-luck if they do not earn as much as they ought, and must bear the burden like their fellow-men if they spend more than they earn. This good sense may corrupt into a cant as others have done, but it is good sense. Marryat—who would appear to have made three thousand pounds or so in 1835, for taking "Mr. Midshipman Easy" and the other two stories, with his copyrights and editorship, he can hardly have made less—was in any case not an example of an ill-paid author. If he had to complain of want of money it must have been because he was a gentleman of extravagant habits, with a fatal weakness for bad investments. To be sure, if an author were to be paid according to the pleasure he has given others, and if "the shop" which makes a profit on selling his work had to render some royalty on it for ever and ever, then indeed was Marryat, together with all those whose work is of the widely-read and lasting order, ill rewarded. But insuperable difficulties bar the road to that ideal. Since paper, printing, and advertisements must be provided, the provider of these necessary things must share ; since the novelist cannot hawk his own goods in a barrow, he must pay somebody to do it for him ; since the world's copyright laws put a limit on the duration of proprietary right in books, there must come a time when they are at any man's disposal to reprint. In the long run the balance of profit must needs be in favour of the shop. To be sure, the nation of authors may console itself by reflecting that it has its revenge. There is much on which the shop makes no gain, first or last.

The first of Marryat's books is one which, for reasons very neatly stated by himself, may stand apart from the others. When he had given it three successors, he thought fit to publish a proclamation on the subject of his work in the *Metropolitan*, and in that document he described "Frank Mildmay" as fairly as any honest critic could do for him.

" 'The Naval Officer' was our first attempt, and it having been our first attempt must be offered in extenuation of its many imperfections ; it was written hastily, and before it was complete we were appointed to a ship. We cared much about our ship and little about our book. The first was diligently taken charge of by ourselves ; the second was left in the hands of others, to get on how it could. Like most bantlings put out to nurse, it did not get on very well. As we happen to be in the communicative vein, it may be as well to remark that being written in the autobiographical style, it was asserted by good-natured friends, and believed in general, that it was a history of the author's own life. Now, without pretending to have been better than we should have been in our earlier days, we do most solemnly assure the public that, had we run the career of vice of the hero of 'The Naval Officer,' at all events, we should have had sufficient sense of shame not to have avowed it. Except the hero and the heroine, and those parts of the work which supply the slight plot of it as a novel, the work in itself is materially true, especially in the narrative of sea adventure, most of which did (to the best of our recollection) occur to the author. . . . The 'confounded licking' we received for our first attempt in the critical notices is probably well known to the reader—at all events we have not forgotten it. Now, with some, this

severe castigation of their first offence would have had
the effect of their never offending again; but we felt
that our punishment was rather too severe; it produced
indignation instead of contrition, and we determined to
write again in spite of all the critics in the universe : and
in the due course of nine months we produced 'The
King's Own.'   In 'The Naval Officer' we had sowed all
our wild oats, we had *paid off* those who had ill-treated
us, and we had no further personality to indulge in."

From which, even if internal evidence were not
enough to prove it, we learn that, between the paying off
of the *Tees* and the commissioning of the *Ariadne*,
Marryat decided to have a general jail delivery of his
old naval enemies, and that the result was " Frank Mildmay; or, The Naval Officer." It cannot be said that
the book is better than its origin. If Marryat had kept
the promise he made in this proclamation of his to the
readers of the *Metropolitan*—if he had re-written this so-
called novel, he might, had he taken the right course,
have made it one of the best of his works. He had
only to make it an autobiography without disguise, to put
in the good as well as the evil of his experience, to take
care to explain everything to his readers, as he could
well have done, and he would have given English
literature a thing altogether unique—a naval memoir.
We are not rich in memoirs, at least, not in good ones.
The English hand is unhappy at that work.   A man has
only to turn to Ludlow, or Sir Philip Warwick, to see
how lamentably little Englishmen of parts who lived
through the most wonderful things could contrive to

bring away with them—how little at least of the life, the colour, the dramatic swing of it all. Of the few we can show, which are not unfit to stand with the Frenchmen, Clarendon, Pepys, Colley Cibber, Evelyn (and four or five others), none were of the sea. "Cochrane's Autobiography" may be quoted against me, but even this, good as it is in places, is drowned in angry denunciations of human wickedness, and demonstrations that this or the other thing ought to have been done by official backsliders, so that what Cochrane did himself is almost crowded out. Besides, it is only a fragment, and then *reste à savoir s'il n'est pas mort.* It has not lived. One may, and must, use it for the history of the man and the time, but who reads it for its intrinsic literary merit? The French seamen have the better of us there. The memoirs of Forbin, of Duguay-Trouin, and even the recently published journal of a much less famous man, Jean Doublet, are capital reading. Marryat might, if he had so pleased, have done a book which would have been to the memoirs of Forbin what the memoirs of Clarendon are to the memoirs of Sully, to adopt the formula dear to Lord Macaulay. He might have done what Sir Walter Scott praised Basil Hall for attempting—have given in autobiographical form a picture of sea life, which would have been interesting, not only to those who already love the subject, but to all who love good reading. He did not so choose. He carried out his mission in another form, and "Frank Mildmay" remained as it first appeared.

That the book was so much of an autobiography was a misfortune for Marryat. He might protest as much as he pleased that he was not Frank Mildmay, and had not

run a career of vice, but the impression left by the book
was and is disagreeable. Why should a man attribute
his own adventures to a tiger? Now, Frank Mildmay
is a tiger—a very insolent, callous, young cub. It shows
Marryat to have been very inexperienced indeed that
he should have made such a mistake. He must have
known that the adventures would be recognized. The
naval world is a small one, and an exclusive. Naval
officers live together by choice on shore as they do by
necessity at sea. Everything written about the profession is talked over, and interpreted, when interpretation
is needed. Every incident in "Frank Mildmay" was no
doubt recognized at once; and when it was found that
the things that had happened to the hero of the story were
the adventures of the author, it is not to be wondered
at that the two were thought to be also identical in
character. Marryat, in fact, committed with himself the
very error of judgment into which Dickens was led with
Leigh Hunt, when he made Harold Skimpole a rascal,
in order to prove that he was not a caricature of his
friend. But there is something more than inexperience
and error of judgment about "The Naval Officer."
Marryat can hardly have seen what a bad fellow he had
drawn. Frank Mildmay has not only those "sins of the
devil," which may be worse, but are more dignified, than
the sins of men—he errs not only by "pride and
rebellion," but he is a mean scamp; and I am afraid that
Marryat did not see it. He was as blind to the faults of
his bantling as Smollett was to the ruffianism of Roderick
Random, or Fielding to the very vulgar inferiority of
Tom Jones. Criticism seems to have opened his eyes,

and little as he liked the lesson, he took the warning; but it was only for a time. Unfortunately he fell back on it. Percival Keene is just such another—a very low fellow, with a kind of wild boar courage. It would appear that Marryat did not see some things as plainly as one could wish he had done. It is unnecessary to insist on the faults of construction in a book which belonged to an altogether bastard genre. What merits it had—and they were sufficient to give promise of a brilliant novelist—were to be repeated in other books much more pleasant, and much more capable of repaying examination.

The other nine books which Marryat published in these seven years were " wholly fictitious in characters, in plot, and in events," to quote his own words. In fact, they were stories, and what truth there is in them was not crudely taken from memory, but adapted and fitted into its place. The essential accuracy of the picture they give of sea life has never been questioned, at least it has never been challenged on serious grounds. It is undoubtedly the case that critics of a certain well-known stamp have been known to complain that no such series of adventures as these stories contain were ever known to occur, and that the daily life of a midshipman is not so amusing as Mr. Easy's, nor so varied as Peter Simple's. A criticism which only amounts to this—that the stories are stories, and not log-books, need hardly be seriously answered. Sailors read them, and always have read them. They are as popular in the American Naval School as they have been among English boys. To the skill with which the stories were built, less justice has been done. It has always, as it were, been taken for granted that Marryat owed everything to his experience as a seaman, and that, except in so far as he had seen things which other men had not seen, he was not of the race of novelists whose work lives. Now this is heresy. In truth, the sea life owes more to Marryat than he to the sea. No one meets Mr. Easy, or Terence O'Brien, or Mr. Chucks, or Mr. Vanslyperken in this commonplace world. He meets something out of which they may be made. Unquestionably his experience was of inestimable value to Marryat—as all exceptional experience is to all novelists. At the very beginning of his career he was complimented by Washington Irving on his good luck. "You have a glorious field before you, and one in which you cannot have many competitors, as so very few unite the author to the sailor." No doubt it was Marryat's happiness that he had so good a Sparta to cultivate—but, after all, the result was primarily due to the skill of the cultivator. Speaking as one who has a full share of the good English taste for reading about the things of the sea, I am inclined to maintain that few kinds of books are more tedious than sea stories which ask to be read and enjoyed simply because they are sea stories. Battle, and storm, and shipwreck may be poured out on you, and yet leave you cold. These things by themselves in fiction are capable of being as tiresome as the once prevalent detective, or now popular religious disputations. To compare the stock sea story with the great books of travel—with Dampier, or with Anson's Voyage, or with Basil Ringrose—would be unfair. We do not need to compare the best of one kind with the worst of another.

But they will not stand reading even with Captain Hacke's dingy little compilation, or with the long-winded journal of Woodes Rogers. The reality of the latter is some compensation for their undoubted dulness. At least in reading them one knows that one is looking at a strange old life told by the men who lived it. When taken by a workman and badly used, the adventures these actual adventurers passed through and recorded become merely. badly used material. A painter was once shown the scrawlings of a youthful prodigy who had been covering paper with pictures of ships and sailors. He was asked whether these works did not show a genius for art. " No," said the judicious artist, " the boy has been reading sea stories, and his head is full of them. He draws because he likes the things, not because he loves drawing." The verdict stated a great critical truth—and, however unpleasant it may be to prodigies to learn that taste and faculty are not identical, and that they must rely on their power of interpreting their subject, and not on the subject itself, it is the case, nevertheless.

Now with Marryat the faculty was always equal to the fusing and managing of the materials. In " Japhet," where he does not touch the sea at all, he has yet contrived to impart life and interest to his puppets and their doings. It may stand by " Con Cregan " in the long list of stories which began with " Guzman de Alfarache," and includes " Moll Flanders " and " Peregrine Pickle." In this case Marryat's best knowledge was not available. and he had to rely on his power of re-using well-worn materials. Where his experience and his ability combined, he attained to a very considerable degree of narrative skill.

Whether he had trained himself by early reading or not (and indeed there is nothing to show that he was a reader), he had early command of a very admirable narrative style. It might be plausibly maintained that this was a heritage among seamen. There is nothing in English literature at once more simple, more manly, more perfectly adequate to its purpose than the language of Dampier. In Marryat's own time this power had not been lost by English seamen. The navy may have been a rough school, but there was nothing in its training which made men unable to use the pen, and use it well. As an example of flowing, and also perfectly unaffected, description, the account of the battle of the Nile, given by Captain Miller, of the *Theseus*, is without fault. It deserves a place of honour in every collection of English letters. The beauty of Collingwood's letters is acknowledged even by those who have thought fit to carp at his character. Marryat brought this style to his literary work, and kept it unchanged to the end. It is a style in which there is no straining. Marryat never had recourse, as his contemporary, Michael Scott, was wont, to capital letters, italics, and broken lines when he wished to impress his readers. He never appears even to have been particularly anxious to impress. When a wreck or a battle comes in his way, it is told as Captain Miller might have told it. Therefore it has its effect, and convinces you, as the narrative of the battle of the Nile does, that the thing described had been seen, had been lived through. The most famous of his passages—the club-hauling of the *Diomede*, the fight with the Russian frigate in "Mr. Midshipman Easy"—the destruction of the French liner at the end of " The King's Own "—are too long for quotation; but in " Peter Simple " there is one which is of not unmanageable length, and which shows the qualities of his writing at their best. It is the account of the hurricane which threw Peter on the coast of St. Pierre :—

" In half an hour I shoved off with the boats. It was now quite dark, and I pulled towards the harbour of St. Pierre. The heat was excessive and unaccountable ; not the slightest breath of wind moved in the heavens, or below ; no clouds to be seen, and the stars were obscured by a sort of mist : there appeared a total stagnation in the elements. The men in the boats pulled off their jackets, for after a few moments' pulling, they could bear them no longer. As we pulled in, the atmosphere became more opaque, and the darkness more intense. We supposed ourselves to be at the mouth of the harbour, but could see nothing, not three yards a-head of the boat. Swinburne, who always went with me, was steering the boat, and I observed to him the unusual appearance of the night.

" ' I've been watching it, sir,' replied Swinburne, ' and I tell you, Mr. Simple, that if we only knew how to find the brig, I would advise you to get on board of her immediately. She'll want all her hands this night, or I'm much mistaken.'

" ' Why do you say so ? ' replied I.

" ' Because I think, nay, I may say that I'm sartain, we'll have a hurricane afore morning. It's not the first time I've cruised in these latitudes. I recollect in '94——'

" But I interrupted him. 'Swinburne, I believe that
you are right. At all events I'll turn back ; perhaps we
may reach the brig before it comes on. She carries a
light, and we can find her out.' I then turned the boat
round, and steered, as near as I could guess, for where
the brig was lying. But we had not pulled out more
than two minutes, before a low moaning was heard in the
atmosphere—now here, now there—and we appeared to be
pulling through solid darkness, if I may use the expression.
Swinburne looked around him, and pointed out on the
starboard bow.

" 'It's a coming, Mr. Simple, sure enough ; many's the
living being that will not rise on its legs to-morrow. See,
sir.'

" I looked, and dark as it was, it appeared as if a sort
of black wall was sweeping along the water right towards
us. The moaning gradually increased to a stunning roar,
and then at once it broke upon us with a noise to which
no thunder can bear a comparison. The sea was perfectly level, but boiling, and covered with a white foam,
so that we appeared in the night to be floating on milk.
The oars were caught by the wind with such force, that
the men were dashed forward under the thwarts, many
of them severely hurt. Fortunately, we pulled with
tholes and pins ; or the gunwales and planks of the boat
would have been wrenched off, and we should have
foundered. The wind soon caught the boat on her
broadside, and, had there been the least sea, would have
inevitably thrown her over ; but Swinburne put the helm
down, and she fell off before the hurricane, darting
through the boiling water at the rate of ten miles an

hour. All hands were aghast; they had recovered their seats, but were obliged to relinquish them, and sit down at the bottom, holding on by the thwarts. The terrific roaring of the hurricane prevented any communication except by gesture. The other boats had disappeared; lighter than ours, they had flown away faster before the sweeping element; but we had not been a minute before the wind, before the sea rose in a most unaccountable manner—it appeared to be by magic.

" Of all the horrors that ever I witnessed, nothing could be compared to the scene of this night. We could see nothing, and heard only the wind, before which we were darting like an arrow, to where we knew not, unless it were to certain death. Swinburne steered the boat, every now and then looking back as the waves increased. In a few minutes we were in a heavy swell, that at one minute bore us all aloft, and at the next almost sheltered us from the hurricane; and now the atmosphere was charged with showers of spray, the wind cutting off the summits of the waves, as if with a knife, and carrying it along with it, as it were, in its arms.

"The boat was filling with water, and appeared to settle down fast. The men baled with their hats in silence, when a large wave culminated over the stern, filling us up to our thwarts. The next moment we all received a shock so violent, that we were jerked from our seats. Swinburne was thrown over my head. Every timber of the boat separated at once, and she appeared to crumble from under us, leaving us floating on the raging waters. We all struck out for our lives, but with little hope of preserving them; but the next wave washed

us on the rocks, against which the boat had already been
hurled. That wave gave life to some, and death to
others. Me, in Heaven's mercy, it preserved: I was
thrown so high up, that I merely scraped against the top
of the rock, breaking two of my ribs. Swinburne, and
eight more, escaped with me, but not unhurt; two had
their legs broken, three had broken arms, and the others
were more or less contused. Swinburne miraculously
received no injury. We had been eighteen in the boat,
of which ten escaped: the others were hurled up at our
feet; and the next morning we found them dreadfully
mangled. One or two had their heads literally
shattered to pieces against the rocks. I felt that I was
saved, and was grateful; but still the hurricane howled—
still the waves were washing over us. I crawled further
up upon the beach, and found Swinburne sitting down
with his eyes directed seaward. He knew me, took my
hand, squeezed it, and then held it in his. For some
moments we remained in this position, when the waves,
which every moment increased in volume, washed up to
us, and obliged us to crawl further up. I then looked
around me: the hurricane continued in its fury, but the
atmosphere was not so dark. I could trace for some
distance the line of the harbour, from the ridge of foam
upon the shore: and for the first time I thought of
O'Brien and the brig. I put my mouth close to Swinburne's ear, and cried out, 'O'Brien!' Swinburne
shook his head, and looked up again at the offing. I
thought whether there was any chance of the brig's
escape. She was certainly six, if not seven miles off,
and the hurricane was not direct on the shore. She

might have a drift of ten miles, perhaps ; but what was that against such tremendous power ? "

Now this might have come straight from another Dampier. There is no attempt to convince you of the force of the hurricane by laborious descriptions of what it looked like. It is shown to be awful by the effect it produces. The sentences go rapidly on. Their very simplicity helps to convey the impression of the sudden- ness and overwhelming fury of the storm. The effect would have been lost if the writer had stopped to talk. The style seems to me to be the perfection of prose, for a tale of adventure—the straightforward, almost colloquial report of one who has gone through it all, carried to its very best—made into literature without being obtrusively literary.

As the style is, so are the stories. A natural tact seems to have told Marryat when he had gone far enough in search of the strange. His heroes lead lives that are possible. He might, if he had chosen, have rivalled Michael Scott's wondrous pirates. Once, indeed, in " Percival Keene," he actually did it, but, as a rule, his pirate is a conceivable good-for-nothing rather cowardly blackguard, such as came in the natural course of things to swing at Kingston or at Execution Dock. Even Cain himself, "The Pirate," is within the bounds of probability as compared with the wondrous Spanish Americans, or astounding Scotch gentlemen of superhuman wickedness, who flourish in " Tom Cringle's Log," and the " Cruise of the *Midge.*" Neither do incidents of the wilder and more horrific kind appear in Marryat's books. There

is nothing in him, for instance, like that scene of the
" *Midge* in the Hornets' nest," which may, by the way, be
commended to the attention of critics who think that
blood and horror have been recently imported into
romance by a generation which is supposed to have been
corrupted by the French taste of the decadence. The
adventures of Marryat's heroes might possibly and even
probably have befallen an officer of his time.

Of construction, except such as was imposed by an
instinctive desire to make the incidents follow one
another in some sort of natural sequence, there is little
or no sign. When, as in "Peter Simple," he tries to fit
one on to his story, it is no addition to the merits of the
book. Who cares a straw for Peter's wicked uncle, for
the changing of the children, or for the unravelling of
the very transparent mystery? It is too obvious that
Marryat took these things at random from the common
fund of the Minerva Press. What he took from
nobody was his fun.

After all, it is this fun which is the living element in
Marryat's work. Wit, or humour of the highest class,
he cannot be said to have possessed, though he was by
no means destitute of the sympathy which is insepa-
rable from all true humour. The sketch of the mate,
Martin, in "Midshipman Easy," is a sufficient defence
against the charge of want of feeling, if, indeed, it had
ever been made. Many who have had a more visible
anxiety to be pathetic than Marryat have failed to draw
so touching a figure as this slight outline of the melancholy officer, in whom the disappointments of years have
crushed all hope, without hardening or souring him.

"No, no," said the mate, when his acting order as lieutenant was brought him as he lay wounded in his hammock, "I knew very well that I never should be made. If it is not confirmed, I may live; but if it is, I am sure to die." And die he does, because hope deferred has dried up the spring of life within him. In the character of Mr. Chucks kindness and fun are mingled. He is respectable in spite of his absurdities, and lovable because of them. In the Dominie in "Jacob Faithful" there is an effort to produce a second Mr. Chucks, but it is not successful. He is too plainly a reminiscence of another Dominie—a fairly well-done copy, but only a copy. For the most part the fun of Marryat belongs to the grotesque order. This, unquestionably, is not the highest. But what is not the highest may yet be genuine, and *that* Marryat's fun, as the world has now recognized for half a century, undoubtedly is. His gallery of "figures of fun" is a long one. Peter Simple in the days before Terence O'Brien made a man of him; Jack Easy before he had been converted from a belief in the equality of all men; in a rougher way his father; Mr. Muddle; and, above all, Mr. Chucks, have an intrinsic comic *vis*. The fun which they make, or which goes on about them, is never mere horse-play. They are not mannikins of the stamp of Smollett's Pallet, created only to be knocked about, and to make grimaces, but possible, and even probable, human beings— a little distorted, a little exaggerated, put frequently into such positions as are more fit for farce than comedy, but not on that account ceasing to be real.

"Mr. Smallsole's violence made Mr. Biggs violent, which made the boatswain's mate violent—and the captain of the forecastle violent also; all which is practically exemplified by philosophy in the laws of motion, communicated from one body to another; and as Mr. Smallsole swore, so did the boatswain swear. Also the boatswain's mate, the captain of the forecastle, and all the men—showing the force of example.

"Mr. Smallsole came forward.

"'Damnation, Mr. Biggs, what the devil are you about? Can't you move here?'

"'As much as we can, sir,' replied the boatswain, 'lumbered as the forecastle is with idlers.' And here Mr. Biggs looked at our hero and Mesty, who were standing against the bulwark.

"'What are you doing here, sir?' cried Mr. Smallsole to our hero.

"'Nothing at all, sir,' replied Jack.

"'Then I'll give you something to do, sir. Go up to the mast-head, and wait there till I call you down. Come, sir, I'll show you the way,' continued the master, walking aft. Jack followed till they were on the quarter-deck.

"'Now, sir, up to the main top gallant masthead; perch yourself upon the cross-trees—up with you.'

"'What am I to go up there for, sir?' inquired Jack.

"'For punishment, sir,' replied the master.

"'What have I done, sir?'

"'No reply, sir—up with you.'

"'If you please, sir,' replied Jack, 'I should wish to argue this point a little.'

" ' Argue the point ! ' roared Mr. Smallsole—'by Jove, I'll teach you to argue the point—away with you, sir.'

" 'If you please, sir,' continued Jack, 'the captain told me that the articles of war were the rules and regulations by which every one in the service was to be guided. Now, sir,' said Jack, 'I have read them over till I know them by heart, and there is not one word of mast-heading in the whole of them.' Here Jack took the articles out of his pocket and unfolded them.

" ' Will you go to the mast-head, sir, or will you not ? ' said Mr. Smallsole.

" ' Will you show me the mast-head in the articles of war, sir ? ' replied Jack ; ' here they are.'

" ' I tell you, sir, to go to the mast-head : if not, I'll be d——d if I don't hoist you up in a bread-bag.'

" ' There's nothing about bread-bags in the articles of war, sir,' replied Jack ; ' but I'll tell you what there is, sir ; ' and Jack commenced reading,—

" ' All flag-officers, and all persons in or belonging to his majesty's ships or vessels of war, being guilty of profane oaths, execrations, drunkenness, uncleanness, or other scandalous actions, in derogation of God's honour, and corruption of good manners, shall incur such punishment as——'

" ' Damnation ! ' cried the master, who was mad with rage, hearing that the whole ship's company were laughing.

" ' No, sir, not damnation,' replied Jack ; ' that's when he's tried above ; but according to the nature and degree of the offence.'

" ' Will you go to the mast-head, sir, or will you not ?

"'If you please,' replied Jack, 'I'd rather not.'

"'Then, sir, consider yourself under an arrest. I'll try you by a court-martial, by God. Go down below, sir.'

"'With the greatest pleasure, sir,' replied Jack; 'that's all right and according to the articles of war, which are to guide us all.' Jack folded up his articles of war, put them into his pocket, and went down into the berth."

Here is farce, but farce which almost borders on comedy. Given Jack Easy with his natural pluck and his absurd training, suddenly put into a man-of-war, and set to reconcile the practice of the service with the ideal picture of it presented by the articles of war, and this is precisely what might be expected to happen. The absurdity always arises from the clash of the characters; and though it be farce, it is farce of the highest order. Rarely does the grotesque lean to the horrible. The death of Mr. Vanslyperken is a case in which it does; but Marryat was, for the most part, content to amuse, and to amuse only.

How well he succeeded we all know. Which of us has not laughed with him ever since we were boys? Mr. Chucks stands between Commodore Trunnion and Mr. Micawber. The scene I have quoted above, and a dozen others, live by the side of Pipe's journey to the garrison with the nymph of the road. The adventures in battle and wreck are very good, but they are not the best. Romance of the brilliant order Marryat did not often try, and when he did, he was at best but moderately successful. He was more of the race of Defoe than of Dumas. But from Defoe, over whom no man ever laughed, he was divided by his love of laughter, and power of drawing it forth. His fun may be often mere animal spirits, but at least it was spontaneous, and was by natural instinct literary. He did not toil and labour to be funny. Even in his most hasty work he would hit off a scene with neat pen-strokes, marking just enough and no more. Take, for instance, the revenue officers in "The Three Cutters." Lieutenant Appleboy and his companions are introduced simply because he had seen them, and as much for his own amusement as his readers. Marryat had seen the types when he was doing preventive work himself in the *Rosario*, and drew them out of his memory when he needed them. Some of his figures were doubtless portraits—all of them had possibly some touch of portraiture. But on his paper they have an interest altogether independent of their originals. There are, as Mr. Saintsbury, speaking of the personalities of Daudet, has said, two ways of drawing portraits in literature. The first is to adapt your sitter into somebody else whom we love for his own sake. The second is to give us an image for which we should care but little if it was not meant for A or B. Of these two methods Marryat took the first. If there was an original to Terence O'Brien we should like to have known him; but, whether or not, we like Terence for his own sake. Was there a boatswain in His Majesty's Service who stood for Mr. Chucks? Possibly; but what then? In Marryat's stories are types as well as individuals. They and their doings have an independent universal truth.

CHAPTER VII

WHEN Marryat was about to start for the United States he gave a reason of some gravity for his proposed trip. The last words of the "Diary on the Continent" propound a serious question : "Do the faults of this people (to wit, the Swiss) arise from the peculiarity of their constitutions, or from the nature of their government? To ascertain this, one must compare them with those who live under similar institutions. I must go to America—that's decided." A biographer of any virtue will desire to be inspired with the Boswellian spirit—to write as loyally as Macaulay did of Addison—but I cannot quite believe that Marryat's visit to America was caused by a sudden passion for the study of comparative politics, and the influence of institutions on national character. A more plausible explanation could be found. It was excellently given by the elder Mr. Weller in the course of some remarks made for the benefit of Mr. Pickwick. To write a book about America was a favourite enterprise with literary persons in those years. Miss Martineau and Mrs. Trollope had just done it, and there was no reason why Marryat should not do it also. A taste for seeing the world may have helped to turn his activity in that direction, and, besides he was, as will be seen, on the lookout for promising speculations, and may have had some thoughts on copyright. Possibly none of these motives were very clear to himself, and he may really have thought he was going to study American institutions.

Moved by sufficient motives, whether the alleged or the unconsciously felt, he did go to America by the packet *Quebec* in 1837, did stay there for two years, and write a book about the States in six volumes, and two series. Of this book it may be said, in a favourite phrase of the writer whom Marryat described as "Mr. Carlisle, the author of 'Sartor Resartus'" (a slip which was dreadfully avenged), that "it is forgetable." Marryat's diary and remarks show that he would have made an excellent newspaper correspondent. He had a faculty for getting up information, a quick eye, and a ready pen. With these qualities a man can easily make "copy" out of a visit to a new country. Indeed, Marryat was no novice at the work, for which his "Diary on the Continent" had pre-pared him. When his six volumes on America are judged as what they were, they are on the whole credit-able. He made the Americans very angry, but that it was never difficult to do. He had provocation to write more bitterly than he did. But whatever may be the merits of, or the excuses for, the thing, it is hardly worth while to return to "newspaper correspondence" at the end of half a century. Unless the correspondent has seen history in the making, and has noted it well so as to become an original authority, he can hardly hope to be read two generations or so later on. The worst of it,

too, is that Marryat saw something which was well worth
recording, and did not record it properly. A large part of
his book is taken up with contradicting Miss Martineau;
and who can rejoice in the refutation of an almost forgotten book by a still more forgotten book?

The incidents of the visit form an interesting passage
in Marryat's life. He reached New York in the midst of
the great financial smash of 1837, and saw the "Empire
City" in all the excitement of panic. He stayed in
America till after the suppression of the Canadian rising,
and himself took part in the fighting. Of course he had
a newspaper controversy—and it was of a kind sufficiently honourable to himself. When he first landed
Marryat seems to have been well received, though with a
certain reserve. By reserve is not to be understood anything so absurd as that he was left alone. On the contrary, he was abundantly overwhelmed with inquiry and
comment. But the Americans were then in the midst of
one of the sorest of their sore fits with foreign comment,
and were (not quite unjustifiably) on their guard against
travellers who came to spy out the land, and make a book
about it. They were not averse to comment, but they
were anxious that it should not only be favourable, but
of exactly that kind of favourableness of which they
approved. Therefore they were intent to know whether
Marryat meant to write about them, and, if so, what he
meant to say. He extricated himself from the difficulty
dexterously enough, and, on the whole, succeeded in keeping on friendly terms with his hosts. As a matter of
course, American copyright institutions, and their effect on
the national character of the publisher, had their share

of his attentions. In this respect, also, his experiences
were pleasing enough in America. He was working in
the intervals of observation. For American consumption
he wrote a play, "The Ocean Waif; or, The Channel
Outlaw," which appeared at a New York theatre; and
he was moreover engaged on "The Phantom Ship." In
1838 he made an arrangement with Messrs. Carey and
Hart to sell them " proof sheets of his 'Diary in
America' and 'Phantom Ship,' a month prior to their
publication in London, for the sum of two thousand two
hundred and fifty dollars ; and provided no one else
published the works in America within thirty days from
the date they issued from their press, a further sum of
two hundred and fifty dollars." Whether pirate enterprise deprived him of the extra sum needed to make up
the round two thousand five hundred, does not appear,
but at least Marryat, with his usual turn for business,
contrived to get something out of America for the
amusement he had given it.

A letter to his mother, pleasant and manly as all his
letters to her were, gives a sufficient picture of the first
part of his stay in America.

" October, 1837.

"My dearest Mother,—I have been so occupied
and I have been moving about so fast that I really have
had time to write to hardly anybody, and I put off a
letter to you till I had a more quiet moment ; but as it
appears that moment was never to come, I now write to
you on board of a steamer on Lake Erie. You have,
of course, heard from the Tuckers [these were his

cousins on his mother's side] that I went up to Boston for a few days to see some of them ; indeed all except Mrs. C—— and Mr. Tucker himself, who was mending his bridge, and could not leave his work ; they were all very kind, but I like poor Mrs. G —— better than any of them.

"I have since been a tour of the lakes, and have travelled some thousand miles. I went up the Hudson, crossed to Saratoga, Trenton Falls, Falls of the Mohawk, Oswego River to Lake Ontario; then to Niagara, Buffalo, and to Lake Erie—to Detroit; from Detroit to Lake St. Clair, and Lake Huron to Mackinan, from Mackinan took a bark canoe, and crossed the Huron, went up the River St. Clair to the Sault Ste Marie, and from thence to Lake Superior. The latter part of the journey, five days in a bark canoe, was very fatiguing, and I was devoured by the mosquitoes; but it has been very interesting, and I have been much gratified. I am now on my return and am bound for Canada, passing by Buffalo and Niagara to Toronto. Since I have been here I have been looking out for a good piece of land, for it more than doubles its value in five or six years, and I have been fortunate in purchasing some very fine land from the Government opposite to Detroit on the Canada side —about 600 acres. I have written to B—— B——, offering to settle him on it, as it is not out of the world, but in very good society. I think it will be worth his while, as in a few years he will be independent. He will however require £300 or so to fit himself out, but that he only need borrow as he will soon be able to pay off. I trust that if he accepts my offer his brother will assist him, and if so, he will do well.

" I am going to Toronto to pay the first instalment, and from there to Montreal, and then I return by Lake Champlain so as to call upon Mrs. C—— at Burlington; and from thence proceed to Bellows Falls to see my Uncle Tucker, who is rather angry with me for not going there before, which I could not. From Bellows Falls I shall return to New York—I do not think by the way of Boston, for they want to give me a public dinner there, and I want to avoid it. At Philadelphia I must be in September for the same purpose, as I accepted the invitation; but I wish they had not paid me the compliment. From Philadelphia I go to Washington to canvass for the international copyright, and then I shall probably go south for the winter.

" The more I see of America the more I feel the necessity of either saying nothing about it, or seeing the whole of it properly. Indeed I am in that situation that I cannot well do otherwise now. It is expected by the Americans, and will also be by the English; and if I do not, they will think I shrink from the task because it is too difficult, which it really is. All I have yet read about America, written by English travellers, is absurd, especially Miss M——'s work : that old woman was blind as well as deaf. I only mean to publish in the form of a diary (but that is the best way); but I will not publish till I have seen all, and can be sure I have not been led into error like others. It is a wonderful country, and not understood by the English now, and only the major part of the Americans. (?) They are very much afraid of me here, although they are very civil; but I do not wonder at it—they have been treated with great ingratitude. **I** at least shall do them justice, without praising them more than they deserve. **No** traveller has yet examined them with the eye of a philosopher, but with all the prejudices of little minds.

" Except a letter from you, I have not received a line from England, which is rather strange. From Kate I have had many letters. I have so many correspondents now—not only at home, but I have a large American correspondence which is too valuable to break off—that I really find I cannot write letter for letter. I have so much to read, so much to write, and so much to think about, that I must be excused. My time is not idly employed, I assure you, although I do not grow thin upon it; but, on the contrary, I think I am fuller than when I left England. I have been so far away these last six weeks that I have heard little English news, except the death of the King and the accession of Princess Victoria. I met Captain V——'s brother the other day who told me that the *Etna* was going home to England in consequence of Captain V——'s health. If so, I may hear something about Frederick, which I have not for a long while. I hope my dear Ellen [a sister] is quite well and happy. My kindest love to her. I will write to her as soon as I can; but it appears to me that I have more to do every day, and I really shall be glad to arrive at Bellows Falls and stay there for a week, if it is only *to take breath*. My journal is already swelled out nearly a volume, and the notes I have taken to work up afterwards will almost double it, and yet I have seen but a small portion of the country. I have picked up two or three good specimens for Joe's mineral collection on

Lake Superior, and some day or another he may get hold of them. Write and tell me all the news. I have not had a line from Mr. Howard or anybody else, which is very strange. The steamboat jogs so that I can hardly write, and I suspect you will hardly be able to read ; but if so, it will take you time to decipher, and therefore will last the longer.

"God bless you, dear mother. A hundred kisses to Ellen, and kind regards to all who care for me.

"Yours ever truly and affectionately,

"F. MARRYAT."

From this letter it may be gathered that in October, 1837, Marryat was in good humour with America, and was seriously thinking of a study of it which should be a possession for ever. America was, on the whole, well pleased with him. He had been civilly received, with a certain reserve as might have been expected, seeing that he was a writing man, who had come with the hardly disguised intention of writing, and after many who had written by no means acceptably ; but still, in spite of this natural wariness, with kindness. He was a good talker and showed it. He had kinsmen in the States who helped him on. Altogether things had gone smoothly with him. The Americans had even been glad to acknowledge his connection with Boston, and some of them had given him a helping hand in that great copyright fight in which the sympathy of the more rightminded has never been denied to the English author, but has also never been of any effect. Unfortunately this very trip to Canada led to a storm which put Marryat for a time into the position of best-abused man on the continent.

At Toronto he was naturally asked to a public dinner, and also naturally requested to speak. In the course of his speech he, again very naturally, took occasion to mention, in a laudatory manner, the cutting out of the *Caroline*, by Lieutenant Drew. This feat had then made some noise in the world. Canada was in a disturbed condition, and the confusion had been fomented by filibustering from the United States territory. The *Caroline* had been fitted out to help the rebels, and had been "cut out" in gallant style from under the guns of Fort Schlosser on the American side of the river, after sharp fighting by a Lieutenant Drew and a body of Canadian volunteers. After capturing the vessel and removing her crew, the Canadians had sent her down over the falls of Niagara. The incident was one of which the loyalists were with good reason proud. As an Englishman, as a naval officer, and as a speaker at a public dinner, Marryat was triply justified in praising " Captain Drew (as he styled him), and his brave comrades who cut out the *Caroline*." Nothing ought to have been a more complete matter of course than that he should propose their health. But Americans were then in a particularly thin-skinned state, even for them. They chose to be very angry with him for doing what any American officer would have done under similar circumstances, at least as loudly. What may be called the spirit of Hannibal Chollop awoke within them, and a chorus of denunciation was begun at once, in the most loud-mouthed and abusive style of American journalism.

Paragraphs headed "More Insolence," and so forth, appeared in abundance. Marryat's books and his effigy were publicly burnt. When he returned from Canada to the States, deputations waited on him, much in the frame of mind of the enlightened citizens who were so indignant when Martin Chuzzlewit offended a free people by coming back from Eden. As a matter of course, any stick was good enough to serve the turn of American journalism. He was accused, among other things, of having "insulted and contradicted, and refused to drink wine" with Henry Clay. The story was, it is needless to say, only a piece of Yankee smartness, but Marryat thought it necessary to appeal to that distinguished politician for a certificate of character, and obtained from him an assurance that their meeting had afforded mutual satisfaction. In short, the whole business was one of those displays of noisy gregarious folly of which our American cousins are occasionally guilty. It was rather more absurd than a recent incident of the same sort, because Marryat was merely a traveller, and was speaking on British territory when he gave the toast which Yankee journalism chose to think offensive. But the old colonial hatred of England (not yet perhaps so entirely dead as after-dinner orators are accustomed to assert) was then full of vigorous life. Americans were wavering between reluctance to plunge into war, and desire to do the old country a damage by helping the rebellious French Canadians. In this divided state of mind they relieved their feelings by howling at Marryat, because he had not "cracked them up accordingly."

Marryat extricated himself from this pass with com-

mendable nerve and dexterity. He faced and soft-
sawdered the deputations. He took the burning of his
books very coolly, went about as before, and finally had
it out with his hosts at a dinner given him at Cincinnati.
The speech, which is far too long to quote, is full of the
manly good sense which the American, when not acting
in the characters of raving journalist or anxious candi-
date, will commonly listen to. Marryat reminded his
hearers that he had spoken in British territory to his
countrymen, and that their own patriotic orators were
not averse to waving the banner habitually, or restrained
from doing so by the knowledge that an Englishman was
present. His hosts being simply American gentlemen,
sitting in their right senses, agreed with him. A somewhat dramatic finish was given to this stage of the incident by Captain J. Pierce, who had been captain of the
American privateer *Ida* when she was taken by the
Newcastle, of which Marryat was then second lieutenant.
Captain Pierce got on his legs to thank Marryat for the
courtesy and good nature he had shown to himself and
other prisoners. "The Wizard of the Sea," as the
American newspapers loved to call him when they were
not in a flaming rage, might consider that, as far as his
hosts at Cincinnati could answer for it, he was cleared
of the charge of insulting the great American people.
Their opinion, like that of the " respectable American,"
in so many other matters, did not avail to stop all
annoyance. Marryat continued to be pestered by abuse,
frequently conveyed in unpaid letters. At last, and
somewhat weakly, in October of 1838, he published a
general protest in the form of a letter to the editors of

the *Louisville Journal*, wherein he denied with much detail that he intended to spy out the barrenness of the land. He was, of course, answered as offensively as might be.

Marryat had perhaps begun by this time to discover that it was not so easy to write of America in a philosophic spirit as he had once thought. To be sure he had laid himself open to annoyance by going to the States at all, and still more by going there with the intention of writing a book.

The Canadian troubles were destined to break into his tour again. In the autumn of 1838 the French population rose in open rebellion, and, as is commonly the fate of insurgents, gained some preliminary successes, which made their final punishment all the more severe. Marryat remembering that he was an English naval officer still on the active list, gave up philosophic inquiry, hurried back to Canada, and volunteered for service under Sir John Colborne. This officer, a veteran of the Great War, and one who had had a distinguished share in winning the battle of Waterloo, made short work of the rising. Marryat saw some fighting once more in his life, and described it briefly in another of his capital letters to his mother.

"MONTREAL, *Dec.* 18, 1838.

"MY DEAREST MOTHER,—Except one letter from B—— B——, it is now nearly four months since I have heard either from England or the Continent; the latter I can in some way account for, at least in my own opinion —still I wish to hear how my little girls are.

"I was going South when I heard of the defeat of St. Denis, and the dangerous position of the provinces of Upper and Lower Canada; and I considered it my duty as an officer to come up and offer my services as a volunteer. I have been with Sir John Colborne, the Commander-in-Chief, ever since, and have just now returned from an expedition of five days against St. Eustache and Grand Brulé, which has ended in the total discomfiture of the rebels, and, I may add, the putting down of the insurrection in both provinces. I little thought when I wrote last that I should have had the bullets whizzing about my ears again so soon. It has been a sad scene of sacrilege, murder, burning, and destroying. All the fights have been in the churches, and they are now burnt to the ground, and strewed with the wasted bodies of the insurgents. War is bad enough, but civil war is dreadful. Thank God, it is all over.

"The winter has just set in; we have been fighting in the deep snow, and crossing rivers with ice thick enough to bear the artillery; we have been always in extremes—at one time our ears and noses frost-bitten by the extreme cold, at others roasting amidst the flames of hundreds of houses. I came out of Grand Brulé after it was all over. I had the greatest difficulty in getting through the fire. I had a sleigh with two grey horses driven *tandem* (as it was too cold to ride the horse the general had offered me), and before I escaped, one side of each of the horses was burnt *brown* and *yellow* before we could force them through; however, the poor animals were more frightened than hurt.

"As I can be of no further use now, I shall return to

America in a few days.   I really wish I could receive a
letter from England.   I feel very much about having no
intelligence.   It will be too late to go South now, and I
think I shall winter quietly at New York, and proceed to
Washington early in the year.

" I really have nothing more to say.   It is hard to fill
a sheet when correspondence is all on one side.   So
give my love to Ellen, and God bless you both.

" Ever your affectionate son,

" F. MARRYAT."

A postscript gives directions to B—— B——, who
appears to have decided to come out and settle on the
desirable piece of land which Marryat had purchased in
Canada.

The American tour was near its end.   Marryat never
made that examination of the South which he had very
justly thought necessary, if he was to obtain a thorough
knowledge of the States.   When he returned to New
York in January, 1839, the country was in no condition
to attract English travellers.   The already existing
hostility to England had been excited to a storm, and
there was copious talk of the tallest kind about war going
on from end to end of the Union.   Everybody was waiting for the President's message and professing to expect
the outbreak of hostilities.   Marryat waited to see what
would come of it all.   The prospect of serious war had
for a moment swept all thought of books out of his mind.
He waited for a summons to join Sir F. Head if his services were further needed in Canada ; but while there was
a prospect that he might again have " a man-of-war on

the ocean," he was in no hurry to run the risk of being shut up in Canada, where the best he could hope for would be a lake command. In a letter from New York to his mother he expresses very explicitly his wishes to serve again, and his hopes of further employment on blue water, and even ends up with one of those growls at the business of book-writing not uncommon among writing men when they happen to be languid, or to have heard bad news. "Mr. Howard" (his former sub-editor no doubt, and the author of "Rattlin the Reefer") "writes me in very bad spirits. He says that I am injured by remaining away from England, and my popularity is on the wane. I laugh at that ; it is very possible people will be ill-natured while I am not able to defend myself ; but what I have done they cannot take from me, and if I wrote no more, I have written quite enough. If I were not rather in want of money I certainly would not write any more, for I am rather tired of it. I should like to disengage myself from the fraternity of authors, and be known in future only in my profession as a good officer and sea-man."

There is about this a ring of manly good sense. Marryat could well afford to laugh at Mr. Howard's croaking, knowing as he did, with his robust self-confidence, that his popularity was in no danger ; that he had it in him to make another popularity if the old was indeed waning. It may well be that his wish to be back in active service was wise. His life might have been longer, and happier, if he had again walked his own quarter-deck. The wish was certainly no vague one, floating idly in his mind. He made plans in Canada, drew maps, and sent home information to the Admiralty in the manifest hope that his exertions would serve him at head-quarters. If war had broken out with the United States it is certain that Marryat, recommended as he was not only by his past services, but by his knowledge of the American coast, would have stood well for employment. But the storm blew over ; the British Empire settled down into peace again, and Marryat remained on shore, driving away with his pen under the pressure of that tyranny which he describes as the state of being "rather in want of money." He left the States early in 1839, and by June of that year was settled in quarters of his own in 8, Duke Street, St. James's.

CHAPTER VIII

THE state of being "rather in want of money" was
to be chronic with Marryat, if we are to judge by
the amount of writing he did during the remaining nine
years of his life. Before very long, indeed, he began to
have very serious reason indeed for complaining of
straitened means. His father's fortune, which must
have been considerable, had been invested in the West
Indies in those golden days at the end of the Great
War, when the languor of Spain, and the ruin of San
Domingo by the negro revolt, had given the English
sugar islands a monopoly of the market for colonial produce. In the forties, however, these happy times had disappeared for ever. Competition and free trade brought
down prices, the abolition of slavery stopped production,
and the value of West Indian property went down with
a run. The Marryat family suffered with the rest of
the world. The novelist had resources which were wanting to his brothers; but then this advantage was com-
pensated, as has been said before, by extravagant and
speculative habits. In 1839 the pinch was not as yet
felt so severely as it was later on. Marryat, immediately
upon his return, went over to Paris for his family, which

had moved thither from Lausanne during his stay in
the States; and, bringing them to England, settled at
8, Duke Street, St. James's. For some four years he led,
as he had hitherto done, a somewhat wandering life.
After a brief year in Duke Street, he moved to Wimbledon House, which had belonged to his father, and was
still occupied by his mother. A short stay there was
succeeded by a brief residence in chambers at 120,
Piccadilly, and then by another year or so of occupation
of a house in Spanish Place, Manchester Square. In
1843 he broke away from London for good, and established himself at his own house at Langham, in Norfolk.

All this restlessness speaks for itself. Men who
possess the faculty of managing their affairs with judgment, or who wish to apply themselves to steady work,
do not run in this way from pillar to post. Once again
I have to remark that much in Marryat's life is left to be
guessed at. It is as well that it should be so. The
indications we possess tell the world all that it is entitled
to learn. There is—though the contrary proposition is
frequently maintained in these days—no inherent right
in the public to be made acquainted with the private
affairs of a gentleman simply because he has done it
the inestimable service of supplying it with readable
books. That Marryat, who has just been found express-
ing a wish to retire from the "fraternity of authors," was
writing himself blind in these years, is a fact which tells
its own tale. Add to this a few indications which Mrs.
Ross Church has thought it right to supply—a brief reference to some family misfortune of which the details are
not given; a complaint in one of Marryat's letters that

somebody, apparently a relation, had suspected him of a wish to borrow money; and an increasing tone of grief and trouble in all his letters—and we have enough to form a general estimate of his position with. More we probably could not learn, and would have no right to hunt up if we could. That Marryat had a difficulty in making both ends meet; that his expedients did not always succeed; that some of them were, too probably, undignified; that the need for them was, at least partly, due to his own mismanagement, are acknowledged facts. We may, and must, be satisfied with them.

It is also easily to be believed that Marryat would enjoy the hard living, and even hard drinking—artistic, literary, and semi-literary—life of his time. Clarkson Stanfield was an intimate friend. Rogers, who was acquainted with everybody, was an acquaintance. With Dickens and Forster his friendship was of long standing, and seems to have remained unbroken. One of the few, and too generally insignificant, letters to her father printed by Mrs. Ross Church, is an invitation to dinner from Dickens, ending with a pleasing promise to give him some hock which would do him good. He was a guest at those merry children's parties which Mr. Forster has described. In his quarters in his various London lodgings we are given to understand that there was much and gay hospitality. Friends were profusely entertained in rooms adorned with furs, trophies, Burmese idols, and weapons—all the miscellaneous curios collected by a sailor and traveller during many wandering hours. In Burmah, Marryat had even made a collection of jewels cut from out of the bodies of slain enemies. The

Burman who has a gem makes an incision in his leg and hides it there, as our sailors discovered more or less to their profit. Unfortunately the curios and the talk are all scattered-and irrecoverable. "It has all vanished like 'air, thin air'"—as Marryat wrote himself of certain common reminiscences to "a lady for whom, to the time of his death, he retained the highest sentiments of friendship and esteem." Marryat's friendships were not all of this enduring kind. "Like most warm-hearted people," as his daughter puts it, "he was quick to take offence, and no one could have decided, after an absence of six months, with whom he was friends and with whom he was not." Eager restlessness is the quality which seems to have been most noticed in him by all his friends. It kept him on the move, not only from house to house, but on excursions to Langham or other parts of England.

The toil which circumstances forced upon Marryat must have greatly aided his natural restlessness in wearing out his life. Steady work and hard work are not necessarily synonymous, and Marryat worked very hard by fits and starts. While in America, and amid all the racket of his tour, he had written "The Phantom Ship," which appeared in 1839. The six volumes of his "Diary in America" followed in the same year. That was not off his hands before he was at work on "Poor Jack." "Masterman Ready," "The Poacher," and "Percival Keene," followed before the end of 1842. Here was an amount of work (six books within five years) which might not be found excessive by the orderly businesslike novelist of to-day, but which must have put a severe strain on a man who wrote at irregular times, but when

actually at it, wrote furiously. It was a distinct aggravation of the burden that his handwriting was very minute.
A man who, having to write a great deal, writes very
small, must either be very sure of his eyesight and his
nerves, or prepared through ignorance or recklessness to
ruin them both. It is, therefore, not to be wondered at
that Marryat's letters between 1839 and 1840 contain
references to the state of his health of a constantly more
melancholy nature. "I shall," he wrote to the same
lady friend in the first of these years, "be at leisure, I
really believe, about the first week in December; but the
second portion of 'America' has been a very tough job.
I am now correcting press (*sic*) of the third volume, and
half of it is done. I hope to be quite finished by the end
of the month, and also to have the other work ready for
publication on the 1st of January; but what with printers,
engravers, stationers, and publishers, I have been much
overworked. I have written and read till my eyes have
been no bigger than a mole's, and my sight about as perfect. I have remained sedentary till I have had *un accès
de bile*, and have been under the hands of the doctor, and
for some days obliged to keep my bed; all owing to want
of air and exercise. Now I am quite well again." Some
two years later the news is much worse, and there is no
mention of complete recovery. "That you may not think
me unkind," he writes again to the same correspondent,
"in refusing your invitation, I must tell you that I am
much worse than I have made myself out in my former
letters. I fell down as if I had been shot a few days ago,
and have been ever since obliged to be very quiet, and am
not permitted to drink anything but water, or undergo the

least excitement, and you would offer me every description in the shape of beauty, mirth, revelry, and feasting, put-ting yourself out of the question! No; for my sins— sins in the shape of three volumes chiefly—and heavy sins, too, I must now submit to mortification and pen-ance. I am positively forbidden to write a line, but you may tell William and Dunny that the little book is finished, and will be out at Easter, when they will be able to read it." Obviously work, and forms of relaxa-tion as wearing as any work, had begun already to ruin a constitution not really robust. Marryat's tendency to break blood vessels had already crippled him when a lieutenant in the navy, and should have warned him that though he might be muscularly powerful, he had no great reserve of constitutional strength to draw on.

The visit to America makes a break in the character as well as in the continuity of Marryat's work. He had said all he had to say about the sea life of his own time, and had to turn elsewhere. The "Diary in America" is perhaps a sign that he thought for a moment of rivalling Captain Basil Hall. If he was indeed tempted to do so, the temptation ceased to be difficult to resist after his return to Europe. The toil of travel, and then of writing out his impressions of travel, had been greater than he had expected, and had produced no equivalent result—either in money or reputation. Mrs. Ross Church states that he received for the "Diary," "on first publishing the manuscript," £1,600. But, according to the same authority, he had received nearly as much for several of his other books in a lump sum, and they con-tinued to bring him in a yearly harvest, whereas the

"Diary" sank at once into the position of a mere book
about America.   In truth, this kind of writing had been
overdone.   There was no longer a market for books of
the Trollope or even the Martineau order.   Everything
had been said about the United States which the public
wanted to hear for the time.   The publishers of the
"Diary" must have discovered that, in taking the
"Diary," they had made the mistake not uncommonly
committed by the trade, and by theatrical managers,
the mistake of overestimating the length of time during
which the public will continue to care for the same thing.
They, doubtless, told Marryat that the taste for stories
was more enduring than the liking for descriptions,
abusive, laudatory, or philosophical, of our American
cousins.   With or without advice of this kind, he
returned to stories, and remained steadily faithful to
them.

"The Phantom Ship," written during the American
tour, differs materially from all the tales which had preceded it, except " Snarley Yow."   It is a romance with a
strong element of *diablerie*.   Possibly because it was not
written in a hurry for the press, it shows more signs of
care in construction than most of the earlier books.
Also, it is an historical romance, and proves that Marryat
had worked at the history of the sea-life—not, doubtless,
very hard, but still to some purpose.   The result makes
one regret that he did not find, or seek for, the leisure
to dig further, and to avail himself of his discoveries.
No great amount of research can have been required to
collect the materials for "The Phantom Ship."   Admiral
Burney's " Discoveries in the South Seas " would alone

have given Marryat all he wanted for this picture of the old Dutch seamanship. Still he brought with him so much knowledge acquired by actual experience that a little was enough. Had he so pleased he might, with the help of Hakluyt, of Monson, and of Sir Richard Hawkins' "Voyage," have given us a picture of the Elizabethan seamen. He might have drawn the "chivalry of the sea," as Washington Irving asked him to do. A "Westward Ho" he would not have written. We should not have had from him (nor have expected) anything equivalent to the dream of Amyas Leigh, or the exquisite speech at the grave of Salvation Yeo. But what he could have done was what Kingsley could not do, and, with the tact of an artist, did not try to do too much. He might have realized the actual sea life of the time— the ships, the seamen, and the seamanship of the past. It was a work in which only a sailor could have succeeded. The pictorial imagination of Kingsley and the conscientious workmanship of Charles Reade alike fail to give reality to their sea scenes. The first was a great artist, and the second an exceedingly clever man with no contemptible share of the imagination of the historian and biographer—the power of seeing the value of materials, of deducing from the report of a thing done the manner of the doing and the nature of the doer. They both worked hard to realize the sea, and yet, if we compare the cruises of the *Rose* and the *Vengeance*, or the fight with the pirates in "Hard Cash," with the "clubhauling" of the *Diomede*, there is a perceptible difference. I am not unaware that one may be unconsciously influenced by the knowledge that Marryat was a seaman, to expect, and see more truth in his pictures than in theirs. Remembering that, however, I still think that his sea scenes differ from Kingsley's, or Reade's, as the thing seen differs from the thing "got up"—with imagination, with insight, with conscientious industry, no doubt,—but still "got up."

In this, and in other ways, Marryat did not do all he might have done. "The Phantom Ship," with "Snarley Yow" which preceded, and the "Privateersman" which followed it, must be taken for what they are worth in place of the possible better. Even so, however, the value of the first of them is considerable. Marryat made a good use of what Leigh Hunt has somewhat hastily decided is the only sea legend. There is no great originality in the incidents. Vanderdecken was made to his hand, and he had German enough—or failing that had translations enough—to supply him with the *diablerie*. But the materials are well used. The story swings along. Philip Vanderdecken, the Pilot Schriften, the greedy Portuguese governor, and the priests have a distinct vitality. Amine is by far his nearest approach to an acceptable heroine; for indeed it must be confessed that this sailor had an altogether maritime ignorance of women, except bumboat women and the ladies of the Hard. The scenes in which his heroines are on the stage are skip. Amine's appearances, however, are not skip. She is a very acceptable heroine of melodrama, good of her kind, with a decided character of her own. The Inquisition scenes in which she is the central figure are the highest point Marryat reached in romance. Very good too are the successive appearances of the Phantom

Ship, done as was commonly the case with Marryat, simply, without straining, without obvious desire to make you shiver. If the last scene of all trenches on the namby pamby, as I am afraid it does, it is preceded by a very good one indeed. Marryat has indicated the loneliness, the weary waiting, the heart-broken striving of Vanderdecken's doomed crew, very sufficiently by the futile effort of the poor mate, who would fain persuade the Portuguese to carry the *Flying Dutchman's* fatal letters home. That Marryat was content to indicate is not the least of his claims to be considered an artist. He knew by instinct, or deduction, the advantage of coming suddenly on his reader. Too many other story-tellers prepare, and accumulate, and pour forth, the materials of the shower (too commonly of adjectives) which is to cause us the *frisson*. We see them doing it, and know what is meant, and, human nature being perverse, hold ourselves steady and refuse to shiver. The princess whose husband could not shiver gave him the emotion by turning the cold water and tittlebats down his back when he was expecting no such shock. If he had seen her filling the tub, putting in the little fishes, and coming to tilt it all over him, there would have been no surprise, and, too probably, he would never have known that delightful sensation.

"Poor Jack," the immediate successor of "The Phantom Ship," is somewhat closer to "Mr. Midshipman Easy," but it, too, is something of an historical study, whether it was deliberately designed to be so or not. Greenwich Hospital has become something very different from the retreat for wounded seamen which

Marryat knew, and his picture of it, somewhat sketchy as it is, will always have the value of a document. The story one need not stop to analyse at any length. Incidents and characters are of the kind familiar with Marryat—not inferior to the average of the others, but not distinguished from them by any very marked characteristics. One piece of fun it does contain not inferior to his best, the immortal apology of the midshipman who had told the master that he was not fit to carry guts to a bear. The palpable absurdity of the incident is on a par with Mr. Easy's amazing use of the Articles of War. "The Poacher" and "Percival Keene," which also belong to these years, both have a flavour of work done only because the author was "rather in want of money." The first is another venture in the same line as "Japhet." The second is the least pleasant, take it for all in all, of the books which bear Marryat's name. It is the only one which had better not be reread in maturer years by him who has read it as a boy. The fun is forced— of the horse-play practical joking kind—and the serious parts are somewhat spoilt by fustian. The negro pirate captain and his crew are good enough for boyish tragedy, but that is not what we expect from Marryat. Finally, too, there is a disagreeable flavour in the book. The hero is a low fellow—not in a healthy human way even, but in a very mean intriguing fashion, and he plays his part in the meanest possible manner.

The one story of these days which could least be spared from Marryat's work is "Masterman Ready." This, the first of his children's books, is also one of the best, perhaps the very best, thing of its kind in English.

It is a child's story in which there is not one word above
the intelligence of the readers it was designed for, one
situation or one character they could not grasp, and yet
it is distinctly literature. It is didactic, and yet there is
no preachment. It is pathetic, and yet it is not mawkish.
It ends with a death-bed scene which is not an offence.
In point of mere cleverness of workmanship it ranks, in
my opinion, first among Marryat's works, and yet it is perfectly simple and unstrained. Marryat was indeed well
qualified to write for children. He had loved their company at all times, and had served a long apprenticeship
in telling stories to his own. The practice had taught
him to avoid the fatal mistake of condescension. An
intelligent child, as even so weighty a writer as Guizot
has remarked, can understand a great deal more than
the duller kind of adult is disposed to allow. It does not
like to be effusively addressed as " my little friend," and
made to see that the kind gentleman or lady who speaks
is intent on improving its mind. "I can't be always
good," said Tommy ; "I'm very hungry ; I want my
dinner." The unsophisticated youthful mind is apt to be
equally direct about its literature. It can't be always
imbibing preachment ; it becomes languid, and wants to
be amused : but it also likes precision of detail, and is
eager to learn the why and how of everything. With
these two rules to guide him—not to be too obtrusively
instructive, and yet to explain every incident as it came,
Marryat wrote a model child's story. Forster was certainly in the right in declaring it to be the most read,
and the most willingly reread, of its class. For its mere
cleverness the book can be enjoyed by the oldest of

readers who is not too dreadfully in earnest. It was no small feat to have taken so well worn a situation as the shipwreck and the desert island, and to have made out of it a book which may stand next to Defoe's. The desertion of the *Pacific* and her passengers by the crew, her wreck, the life on the island, the fight with the savages, and the rescue, are as probable, they follow one another as naturally, as the events in the life of Robinson Crusoe. Marryat had too much tact and knowledge to fall into the extravagances of the "Swiss Family Robinson." The beasts and plants of the island are not an impossible collection of the flora and fauna of three continents. Then, too, the book contains two of Marryat's very best characters. Masterman Ready is an ideal old sailor, brave, modest, kind, helpful, able to turn his hand to anything, and to do it well, yet, withal, no mere bundle of abstract virtues, but a most credible human being— such a man as might have been formed by such a life. Very different, but equally good, is Master Tommy Seagrave, the ideal of greedy, naughty boys. Tommy's ever vigorous appetite and irrepressible passion for making a noise, for meddling with everything, for trying everything, for spoiling everything, are as perfect in their way as the meek heroism of Masterman Ready. At the end, the collision of the two produces very genuine tragedy. Master Tommy was just the boy who would have emptied the water-butt, under pretext of bringing water from the well, and would have accepted the very undeserved praise bestowed on his zeal without the faintest scruple. The consequences of his bad behaviour are absolutely natural and inevitable. That Masterman Ready should have met his death through Master Tommy was an artistic stroke of the highest merit. And Marryat tells it all with a calm detachment which might reduce the average Russian novelist to despair. He is not wroth with Tommy. He accepts him as inevitable, and only describes him with a calm artistic precision, simply as the type of "The Boy." Then, too, consider the final no-repentance and escape of Tommy. He howled for water and got it, and Masterman Ready died that he might have it. The little wretch never knew what mischief he had done. He sailed away to Sydney with an excellent appetite, and as long as he had enough to eat, and things to break, was no doubt perfectly happy. There is a something colossal in the truth, and the artistic calmness of the whole story.

While Marryat was at work on "The Poacher," he had a slight literary skirmish—not unworthy of notice as a proof that certain things are unchanging in the literary world. The story appeared in *The Era* in weekly numbers. One of those remarkable persons, who, in every successive generation, find it necessary to make a protest in favour of the dignity of literature, and whose idea of dignity commonly is that literature can only be good when it appears in a certain way and at a certain price, fell foul of Marryat for choosing this low method of publication. This egregious person wrote in *Fraser*, and very gratuitously attacked Marryat, in the course of some remarks on Harrison Ainsworth, in the following "slashing" style : "If writing monthly fragments threatened to deteriorate Mr. Ainsworth's productions, what must be the result of this *hebdomadal* habit? Captain Marryat, we are sorry to see, has taken to the same line. Both these popular authors may rely on our warning, that they will live to see their laurels fade unless they more carefully cultivate a spirit of *self-respect.* That which was venial in a miserable starveling of Grub Street is *perfectly disgusting* in the extravagantly paid novelists of these days—the *caressed* of generous booksellers. Mr. Ainsworth and Captain Marryat ought to disdain such *pitiful peddling.* Let them eschew it without delay."

These were very bitter words, but the only influence they had on Marryat was to provoke him to show that he could do the single-stick style as well as the *Fraser* men themselves. With less wit, but more good humour than Thackeray, he, too, wrote his Essay on Thunder and Small Beer. He pointed out that there is no necessary connection between the manner of publication and the method of composition of a book, and even made quite respectable fun of *Fraser's* pedantry. "In the paragraph," he says, "which I have quoted there is an implication on your part which I cannot pass over without comment. You appear to set up a standard of *precedency* and *rank* in literature, founded upon the rarity or frequency of an author's appearing before the public, the scale descending from the 'caressed of generous publishers' to the 'starveling of Grub Street'—the former, by your implication, constituting the *aristocracy* and the latter the *profanum vulgus* of the quill. Now although it is a fact that the larger and nobler animals of creation produce but slowly, while the lesser, such as rabbits, rats, and mice, are remarkable for their fecundity ; I do not think that the comparison will hold good as to the breeding of

brains; and to prove it, let us examine— if this argument
by implication of yours is good—at what grades upon
the scale it would place the writers of the present day."
By applying "this argument by implication " in a rigid
fashion, Marryat has no difficulty in showing that "my
Lady —— anybody," who produces one novel a year, is
necessarily twice as great a writer as Hook or James who
produces two, and twelve times as great as the *Fraser* man
himself, whose production is monthly. The reasoning is
burlesquely fallacious, but it was meant to be so. Marryat
spoke with more gravity, and more point too, when he
urged that he was doing a good work by spreading his
story "among the lower classes, who, until lately (and
the chief credit of the alteration is due to Mr. Dickens),
had hardly an idea of such recreation."

"In a moral point of view I hold that I am right.
We are educating the lower classes; generations have
sprung up who can read and write; and may I inquire
what it is they have to read, in the way of amusement?—
for I speak not of the Bible, which is for private examination. They have scarcely anything but the weekly
newspapers, and as they cannot command amusement,
they prefer those which create the most excitement; and
this I believe to be the cause of the great circulation of
The Weekly Despatch, which has but too well succeeded
in demoralizing the public, in creating disaffection and
ill-will towards the Government, and assisting the ne-
farious views of demagogues, and chartists. It is certain
that men would rather laugh than cry—would rather be
amused than rendered gloomy and discontented—would
sooner dwell upon the joys and sorrows of others, in a

tale of fiction, than brood over their supposed wrongs.
If I put good and wholesome food (and, as I trust, sound
moral) before the lower classes, they will eventually
eschew that which is coarse and disgusting, which is only
resorted to because no better is supplied. Our weekly
newspapers are at present little better than records of
immorality and crime, and the effect which arises from
having no other matter to read and comment on, is of
serious injury to the morality of the country. . . . I
consider, therefore, that in writing for the amusement
and instruction of the poor man, I am doing that which
has been but too much neglected —that I am serving my
country, and you surely will agree with me that to do so
is not *infra dig.* in the proudest Englishman : and, as a
Conservative, you should commmend, rather than stigma-
tise my endeavours in the manner which you have so
hastily done."

The intention and the argument here are better than
the style.   Marryat was better at narrative than exposi-
tion, and could at times be as free with the relative
pronouns as that distinguished officer, Captain Rawdon
Crawley.   The confidence Marryat, in common with
most of his contemporaries, reposed in the influence of
wholesome amusement was doubtless excessive.   It has
not been found that when the " poor man " [or other
reader for that matter], has a choice of Hercules given
him between good literature and bad, he will cleave to
the first and reject the last.   Also, there is a candid
confession of the faith "that there is nothing like
leather" in Marryat's confidence that good weekly stories
would soothe the discontent which was seething in Eng-

land before 1848. But in spite of slips of grammar, optimism, and over-confidence, Marryat's answer to the priggery in *Fraser* is a creditable manifesto. To desire to kill the trash of *The Weekly Despatch* was at least a respectable ambition, and a man has a good right to believe in his causes, and his weapons.

CHAPTER IX

LANGHAM, to which Marryat betook himself for good in 1843, had been in his possession for some thirteen years. Its history, as far as he was concerned, may be taken to have been characteristic of the man. He acquired it, according to Mrs. Ross Church, by exchange—having "swapped" it, after dinner and copious champagne, against Sussex House, Hammersmith. From that period it had been an interesting but unprofitable possession to him. Before he left for America he had already had occasion to complain of the difficulty of getting rent. A tenant had been expelled, and replaced by another of the fairest character. But appearances had proved delusive. Langham had been all along more of a burden than a profit to its owner. In 1843 he seems to have decided to see what he could do with it himself. A passage in his fragmentary life of Lord Napier, quoted by his daughter, shows that he shared to the full the common delusion of men, and the especial delusion of sailors, that it is easy to manage a small property. In this pleasing but fatal belief he set out to see what he could do with the 700 acres of the estate himself. Again I have to acknowledge my inability to

give any account of the motives for this sudden (for it
appears to have been sudden) decision. Considerations
of economy were doubtless of weight with him. The
fall in the value of West Indian property had, as has
been said, hit him hard. The demands on his purse
were as heavy as ever—indeed, to judge from a somewhat
plaintive reference in one of his letters—even heavier.
He speaks in this place of actions brought by tradesmen
to recover money for goods supplied to his sons Frederick
and Frank—from which we may conclude that the young
men had inherited their share of the paternal faculty for
spending money. Their father was driven to express the
wish that the value of this necessary was taught in schools.
Neither at school nor at home do the young Marryats
appear to have gained this knowledge, and in those years
the navy, which they had both entered, was no school of
thrift. Doubtless they were among the causes which first
induced Captain Marryat to betake himself to the
country, and then kept him hard at work when he was
there.

Langham is in the northern division of Norfolk, half-
way between Wells-next-the-Sea and Holt. The Manor
House, says Mrs. Ross Church, "without having any
great architectural pretensions, had a certain unconven-
tional prettiness of its own. It was a cottage in the
Elizabethan style, built after the model of one at Virginia
Water belonging to his late Majesty, George IV., with
latticed windows opening on to flights of stone steps
ornamented with vases of flowers, and leading down
from the long narrow dining-room, where (surrounded
by Clarkson Stanfield's illustrations of 'Poor Jack,' with

which the walls were clothed) Captain Marryat composed his later works, to the lawn behind. The house was thatched and gabled, and its pinkish white walls and round porch were covered with roses and ivy, which in some parts climbed as high as the roof itself." When Marryat came down to examine his property with an intention of living on it, he found it suffering from all the evils which commonly fall upon the property of absentee landlords. The tenant of the larger of the two farms into which the estate was divided had not only mismanaged his land. Having the house itself at his mercy, he had turned the drawing-room into a common lodging-house, in which tramps and other necessitous persons could have a bed for the modest sum of two-pence a night. The windows were smashed or unclosed, and the birds of the air had built their nests in the rooms. This state of neglect was soon changed for the better, and Langham Manor became habitable.

In it Marryat sat down during the last five years of his life, to show in practice the soundness of his theory touching the fitness of sailors for the management of small properties. It will surprise few to learn that the result only proved once more that small properties are not so easily forced to yield a profit. Even before actually coming to live on the estate, Marryat had tried various speculations with his land. The results of his efforts, personal and vicarious, are illustrated in his daughter's "Life" by the following extracts, taken at random from his farm accounts.

		£	s.	d.
1842.	Total receipts	154	2	9
	Expenditure	1637	0	6
1846.	Total receipts	898	12	6
	Expenditure	2023	10	8

It will be seen that the balance was less heavily against Marryat in '46 when he was present, than in '42 when he could only look on from afar. Even in these cases the master's eye is of value. It is better to lose on your own ventures than to be robbed all round, and in so far Marryat no doubt gained by living on his land. In 1845 he even secured some compensation for the damage done to his house and property by the dishonest tenant—at least the courts decided that compensation should be paid him. After a lawsuit, an unsuccessful effort at compromise, and (Marryat declares) much hard swearing by his opponent, he was awarded £150. Whether he ever got it is a question, for the tenant seems to have been meditating bankruptcy immediately afterwards. The end of the business is wrapt up in mystery. On the whole, one can quite believe that the Captain's "agricultural vagaries appeared almost like insanity to those steady plodding minds that could not understand that a man may have genius, and no common sense." Quite credible, too, is it that Marryat was very particularly proud of his common sense, and " would have been very much hurt " if any man had doubted his claim to possess it in an eminent degree. If there is anything of which the more flighty kind of speculator is firmly persuaded, it is of his practical faculty and sober good sense. It is very characteristic that in all Marryat's stories for children, and in touches scattered over his earlier works, there are proofs of a taste for thinking about matters of business, and for constructing plausible narratives of profitable investments of money and labour. It would seem that, among writing men (and not among them only) this taste is an infallible sign of a natural incapacity to acquire three pennyworth of anything for less than eighteen pence. Balzac had it, and he never could keep his fingers off a losing speculation. Marryat is so exact about sums of money, and has such a turn for showing how profits are to be made, that we are quite prepared to hear of him bursting into his brother's room at 3 o'clock a.m., with splendid schemes for draining the marshes of Clay-by-the-Sea, and thereby realizing wealth beyond the dreams of avarice. It follows as a matter of course that his only surviving son, Frank, found Langham a worthless inheritance.

It is at this period of his life that we can obtain the best, and, indeed, almost the only personal view of Marryat. Of the last years of his life at Langham, Mrs. Ross Church speaks from memory, and her evidence has independent support. The picture we obtain is in the main pleasant, though it is sufficiently clear that Marryat was not exactly an angel. "Many people," says his daughter, "have asked whether Captain Marryat, when at home, was not 'very funny.' No, decidedly not. In society, with new topics to discuss, and other wits about him on which to sharpen his own—or, like flint and steel, to emit sparks by friction—he was as gay and humorous as the best of them; but at home he was always a thoughtful, and, at times, a very grave man; for he was not exempt from those ills that all flesh is heir to, and had his sorrows and his difficulties and moments of depression like the rest of us. At such times it was dangerous to thwart or disturb him, for he was a man of strong passions and indomitable determination; but, whoever felt the effects of his moods of perplexity or disappointment, his children never did." Mrs. Ross Church must forgive it if this description reminds me more than a little of a certificate to character I once heard given to a British skipper, a mahogany-faced man of immense strength and violence, in the office of one of Her Majesty's consuls, in a Mediterranean port. This gallant seaman had been summoned by one of his men for assault and battery. He confessed the beating, but denied that it had been so aggravated as the plaintiff alleged. Moreover he pleaded provocation, and called up his boatswain as a witness to character. The boatswain, an honest-looking rather chuckle-headed fellow, was obviously torn by conflicting desires. He did not wish to displease his captain, and yet he did not wish to tell lies which would go against his comrade. Nothing definite could be got out of him while in the presence of the parties. When asked in confidence (and in an outer office) what the truth of the matter was, he answered, "Why, you see, sir, it's just this—the captain he's a very good sort of man as long as he has everything his own way—but when he's crossed he clears the place."

It may be taken as proved, then, that Marryat had in abundance that kind of good nature which is displayed when the owner is pleased and happy—of which this may at least be said, that it is vastly superior to no good nature at all. Moreover, we have to consider what things it was that made him displeased and unhappy. Mrs. Ross Church's qualification to the character just quoted shows that he did not entirely hang his fiddle up when he came home. To his children " he was a most indulgent father and friend, caring little what escapades they indulged in so long as they were not afraid to tell the truth. 'Tell truth and shame the devil' was a quotation constantly on his lips ; and he always upheld falsehood and cowardice as the two worst vices of mankind. He never permitted anything to be locked or hidden away from his children, who were allowed to indulge their appetites at their own discretion ; nor were they ever banished from the apartments which he occupied. Even whilst he was writing, they would pass freely in and out of the room, putting any questions to him that occurred to them, and the worst rebuke they ever encountered was the short determined order, 'Cease your prattle, child, and leave the room,' an order that was immediately obeyed. For with all his indulgence of them, Captain Marryat took care to impress one fact upon his children—that his word was law."

The children were aware that they were dealing with a parent not incapable of getting in a rage, and therefore stopped in time—which is one of the many advantages of not possessing a too equable temper. These collisions of theirs with the sovereign authority at Langham cannot, however, have been frequent, as this further quotation from Mrs. Ross Church will show : "The long-expected governess [there were great negotiations over the engagement of this official], when eventually secured and transplanted to Langham, was not received by the children, who had been accustomed to have their own way in everything, with much enthusiasm; and their father was the friend to whom they invariably appealed for protection against her authority. Captain Marryat had rather an original plan with respect to punishment and reward. He kept a quantity of small articles for presents in his secretary, and at the termination of each week the children, and governess armed with a report of their general behaviour, were ushered with much solemnity into the library to render up an account. Those who had behaved well during the preceding seven days received a prize, because they had been so good; and those who had behaved ill also received one, in hopes that they would never be naughty again. The governess was also presented with a gift, that her criticism on the justice of the transaction might be disarmed. Thus all parties left the room perfectly satisfied; an end which, Captain Marryat used to observe, it required some diplomacy to attain. The governess was in the habit of restraining the children's thoughtlessness by imposition of fines or lessons when they tore their clothes; but, as tearing their clothes was an event of daily occurrence, the punishment became rather heavy; and one of the younger ones, having made a large rent in a new frock, ran in dismay to her father in order to consult him how best to escape the impending doom. Captain Marryat, without any regard to the future of the garment in question, took hold of the rent and tore off the whole lower

part of the skirt. 'Tell her *I* did it,' he said in explanation as he walked away." This story, which had pre-
viously made its appearance in an article in the *Cornhill Magazine*, is supported there by the general assertion
that whenever any of the young Marryats required punishment they were doubly petted for the rest of the day.
" It seemed as if no amount of indulgence was thought
too much for compensation; like the jam to take the
taste of the physic out of the mouth."

Persons who make a serious study of the art of training
children may not all agree that a system which recommended courage by giving them nothing to fear, incul-
cated the love of truth by making it safe and pleasant to
tell it, and developed the moral virtues by unlimited
indulgence, was one to be held up as a model to fathers.
No doubt, however, it was abundantly pleasant for the
children, and it may readily be believed that Captain
Marryat was loved by his own house. With his children
he lived on terms of affectionate freedom, making them
his companions, and even training them to play piquet,
for which scientific game he had a great affection, in
order that they might share with him in all things.

For animals, too, he had a genuine but not a maudlin
affection. His dogs and his pony Dumpling figure much
in the accounts given of his last years. His favourite
bull, Ben Brace, was kept tethered opposite the window
of the room in which he wrote. It is a good sign
of his genuine kindness for animals that he seems to
have been made rather impatient by the gushing talk
about them, and the wondrous tales of their intelligence,
which are (in the opinion of some) nearly the most

nauseous of all forms of twaddle. We have it on his own authority that he joined Theodore Hook in inventing outrageous stories about the intelligence of animals, and palming them off on the too credulous popular naturalist. To his men Marryat seems to have been a kind master. He at least gave them copious feasts on proper occasions. "All the men who were on the farm," he tells his god-daughter, "were invited to a Christmas dinner in the kitchen, and they sat down two-and-twenty at the table in the servants' hall, and were waited upon by our own servants. They had two large pieces of roast beef, and a boiled leg of pork; four dishes of Norfolk dumplings; two large meat pies; two geese, eight ducks, and eight widgeon; and after that they had four large plum puddings." This, with "plenty of strong beer," which was also duly supplied, made, as Marryat seems to have felt with pardonable satisfaction, a feed likely to be remembered by the two-and-twenty farm hands. He was not so original as he perhaps thought himself, or as some have supposed him to have been, in employing an ex-poacher, one Barnes, as gamekeeper. That particular kind of thief had often been set to catch the other thieves before Captain Marryat went to live at Langham. The poacher who is not merely the paid hand of a London poulterer is commonly enough not such a bad fellow, and when he is allowed to combine his sporting tastes with a regular salary, and a position of some authority, is capable of doing fairly well. In this case whatever risk Marryat ran was justified by the result. Barnes proved not only a good servant to him, but is said to have been a loyal follower to his son Frank when he emigrated to California.

Here, on his own land, surrounded by his family, Marryat spent what were, doubtless, not the least happy years of his life. An occasional friend from London found the ex-*viveur* and dandy in velveteen shooting jacket and coloured trousers, turning out at five in the morning, trotting about his farm on Dumpling, attentive to scientific farming, and invincible in hope of profit from that deceptive venture. For company, he had his romps with his children, his game of piquet, and an occasional, or even frequent, visit from Lieutenant Thomas, of the coastguard station at Morston. The two old seamen met, and talked of the rapid progress of the service to the d——, as old seamen have done from the beginning, and will do to the end of time. From the outer world came requests for work from editors, suggestions that he should take up this subject or the other, and at times invitations to come up and take part in farewell dinners to Macready or to Dickens. These last he steadily declined. Except during a few brief visits to London on matters of business, he remained fixed at Langham till the disease which proved fatal drove him up to town in search of better medical help than he could obtain in Norfolk.

He has himself described the work of these last years in a letter to Forster, who had written in 1845 to Marryat, suggesting that he should give "a month or two to a short biography, of about a volume ; something of the size and manner of Southey's ' Nelson,' and the subject ' Collingwood.' " Marryat thought it over, but declined, giving, among other reasons, this : " That I have lately taken to a different style of writing, that is, for young people.

My former productions, like all novels, have had their day, and for the present, at least, will sell no more; but it is not so with the *juveniles;* they have an annual demand, and become *a little income* to me; which I infinitely prefer to receiving any sum in a mass, which very soon disappears somehow or other." Marryat justified his unwillingness to write the life of Collingwood by other than business reasons. " I should like," he told Forster, " to write about Collingwood, but if I were to write it in anything like a stipulated time I should not do it well. Biography is most difficult writing, and requires more time and thought than any original composition, and if I take it up I must be free as air." In addition to this (justly high) estimate of the difficulty and dignity of biography, Marryat, with sound critical judgment, decided that Collingwood was not a proper subject. There is not enough known or to be known about him. So much of his work was done as a subordinate under St. Vincent or Nelson. With them he was always in the second place at best, and when he reached great independent command, the heroic days of the naval war were over, and there was little for him to do beyond duties of a mainly routine character, performed in the midst of chronic illness. It is a pity perhaps that Marryat did not devote some part of his work to naval biography, but he would hardly have made a real success with Collingwood. For Forster himself, Marryat wrote a series of letters to the *Examiner* on the "Condition of England Question," or that part of England which he saw about him in Norfolk. " I have," he wrote to Forster, " been amusing myself with putting together my thoughts and knowledge of the con-

dition of the agricultural class—I mean the common
labourer principally—and I believe I know more of the
subject than anything I have seen in print. What I can
say is from personal knowledge. I was thinking of
writing some letters to Peel as a Norfolk farmer, 'The
Poor Man *versus* Sir Robert Peel.' It would not do to
put my name to them as they would be anything but
Conservative, but they would be the *truth*." It was not
Marryat's destiny to be a politician, and his opinion of
Sir Robert Peel is perhaps not very valuable. His own
political activity was not particularly consistent, for he
appears to have swayed from Reformer to Conservative,
and back again, but it may be noted that he ended by
sharing that dislike of the leader who always led his followers to surrender which was so widely felt in Peel's
last days.

His main work was always his stories for children.
Five of these belong to the Langham period—"The
Narrative of the Travels and Adventures of Monsieur
Violet," "The Settlers in Canada," "The Mission,"
"The Children of the New Forest," and "The Little
Savage." There may be some doubt whether the first
ought to come under this heading. Marryat did not
consider it a child's story himself; but if it is not *that*
one has some difficulty in deciding what it was. The
materials were, Mrs. Ross Church says, supplied by a
young Frenchman, named Lasalles, who turned up at
Langham, and astonished the neighbourhood by lassoing
cattle and doing other barbarous feats. The matter
supplied by this amusing adventurer was "licked into
shape" by Marryat. This account of the origin of the

book is certainly borne out by its contents. It is a
somewhat rambling story of adventure among the Red
Men, starting from an improbability, and ending somewhat abruptly. No small part of it consists of an account
of the early Mormons, and has sadly the air of padding.
On the whole, it has much more the look of a collection
of notes for a tale of adventure than anything else, and
has always been one of the least read, if not entirely the
least read, of the books which bear Marryat's name. Of
" The Mission " its author gave an exact account in a
letter to his friend Mrs. S——: " It is composed of
scenes and descriptions of Africa in a journey to the
Northward from the Cape of Good Hope—full of lions,
rhinoceroses, and all manner of adventures, interspersed
with a little common sense here and there, and inter-
woven with the history of the settlement of the Cape up
to 1828—written for young people of course, and, therefore trifling, but amusing." " The Mission," although
this promising sketch of it is strictly correct, has not
been much more popular than " Monsieur Violet," and
the reason is obvious enough. It is not so much
a story as a series of unconnected, or very loosely
connected, incidents ; and moreover, it contains what
any right-minded boy could only regard as a cruel
"sell." The hero starts forth to clear up the fate of
a relative—a lady who has been wrecked on the Caffre
coast many years before. It is not known for certain
whether she was drowned or died on shore, and a fear has
always existed that she survived as a prisoner among the
natives, and had grown up to be the wife of some Caffre
chief, and bear him young barbarians in his kraal—a fate

which it is believed did actually befall the daughters of
an English officer, who were wrecked on that coast on
their way back from India. He goes on, hears of a
renowned chief, whose mother was an Englishwoman,
finds him, and then discovers that it was another shipwrecked lady, who had the happiness to produce a half-
bred hero in that distant region. His own relative has
certainly perished. Now this is cruel. It was not worth
while to go so far to learn so little, and the feeling of disappointment caused is too acute. Marryat made a fatal
mistake when he overlooked the possibilities of the situation. For the rest, it is a pity he did, because the
background of the story is particularly good. Marryat
seems to have obtained a very clear idea of the Cape,
which he must have visited during his service in the
South Atlantic. His hunting adventures, his Zulu war-
riors, his Dutch Boers, and Hottentot boys are distinctly
good. There is even a touch of something grandiose in
the references to the invaders from the North, who were
then pressing down on Caffraria. They weigh in an imposing fashion on the fortunes of the adventurers in
"The Mission." It is somewhat unfair to look at it
all now, when these materials have again been made
popular. But good as it is of its kind, the book has a
feeble, aimless look, simply from want of satisfactory
ending.

Of the three children's stories which remain—"The
Settlers," "The Children of the New Forest," and " The
Little Savage "—the second is most likely to be interesting to children, and the last is, in part at least, the most
original. There is something rather gruesome in the

picture of the child born on a desert island, and growing up by the side of a ruffian who bullies him. The natural savagery of the human animal is developed in him unchecked, and Marryat has shown some power in the scenes in which the boy discovers the helplessness of his companion, who has been blinded by a flash of lightning, and then turns on him with cool ferocity. But the promise of the beginning is not kept. "The Little Savage" becomes didactic—full of repetitions—and ends by being more than a little tiresome. On the whole, after all, "The Children" is better. Our old friends, the Cavaliers and Roundheads, are less new than "The Little Savage," but they last out more briskly. It is a child's story of merit—nothing more—and the historical erudition of it, if somewhat shallow, is on a level with that of more pretentious books. "The Privateersman" has a certain interest as being the last of Marryat's sea stories, and as a picture, or at least a rough sketch, of the strange old privateer life of which "The Voyages and Cruises of Commodore Walker" is almost our only record from the inside. It is not a pleasant book, or a strong. Moreover, Marryat puts his hero in the very most ignoble position any hero was ever in. It may be safely laid down as a rule that under no conditions ought a gentleman to desert a woman in a forest full of Red American Indians. It is one of those things which a gentleman cannot do. Now the hero of "The Privateersman" does it—and the deduction is obvious. The story has touches which remind one of "Colonel Jack," but it is too clearly a book written simply to fill space in a magazine. Marryat's fun had gone when he wrote it for Harrison Ainsworth and *The New Monthly Magazine.* "Valerie," a species of Japhet in petticoats, is not even all Marryat's, and was, in any case, written when he was slowly dying.

CHAPTER X.

THE weakness which proved fatal to Marryat had shown itself while he was still a young lieutenant in the West Indies. He had then been invalided home for rupture of a blood vessel in the lungs, and a military doctor "also certified to his tendency to 'hœmoptysis,' and prophesied that, without great care, 'the most dangerous and perhaps fatal results' would be the consequence" of rashness. The danger had passed at that time—had probably been avoided by the use of care—and for many years Marryat had to all appearance been a very robust man. He was of the best possible height and build for strength. . He was some five feet ten inches high, with broad deep chest, and his muscular force was exceptionally great. His portrait, as far as it can be judged of from the engraving prefixed to "Frank Mildmay," gives the impression of a man of boundless energy, open-faced, alert, and keen eyed. He was black-haired with blue eyes, and his beard grew so thick and so fast that he was compelled to shave twice a day. When he came to Langham, in 1843, his strength was apparently still unbroken, and he might appear sure of long years of health and capacity for work. But it is clear that there

was more appearance than reality in his strength. When
a man has turned fifty he begins to suffer for the unwis-
dom of former years. Marryat, unfortunately, had never
given himself any quarter. He had spared himself no
burden a man can lay upon his strength. He had played
and worked to excess, had lived in a whirl of nervous
excitement, had spent beyond his means in constitution
as well as in purse. If he had not spent his summer
while it was May—at least he had run through it far too
soon. Langham, which might have given him rest, was
only the scene of more nervous excitement, more
strenuous work. In 1847 the end began. In August of
that year he speaks, in a letter to his sister, of having
recently ruptured two blood vessels. The following
letter shows that the accident occurred in London, but
Marryat returned to Langham, and remained there till
the want of medical advice likely to inspire more confidence than a country doctor's drove him to London
again. He remained at his mother's house at Wimbledon
for two months, and from it wrote to Lord Auckland,
then at the Admiralty, on December 14th.

" My Lord,—When I had the honour of an audience
with you, in July last, your lordship's reception was so
mortifying to me that, from excitement and annoyance,
after I left you I ruptured a blood vessel, which has now
for nearly five months laid me on a bed of sickness.

" I will pass over much that irritated and vexed me,
and refer to one point only. When I pointed out to
your lordship the repeated marks of approbation
awarded to Captain Chads—and the neglect with which

my applications had been received by the Admiralty during so long a period of application---your reply was 'That you could not admit such parallels to be drawn, as Captain Chads was a highly distinguished officer,' thereby implying that my claims were not to be considered in the same light.

"I trust to be able to prove to your lordship that I was justified in pointing out the difference in the treatment of Captain Chads and myself. The fact is that there are no two officers who have so completely run neck and neck in the service, if I may use the expression. If your lordship will be pleased to examine our respective services, previous to the Burmah War, I trust that you will admit that mine have been as creditable as those of that officer; and I may here take the liberty of pointing out to your lordship that Sir G. Cockburn thought proper to make a special mention relative to both our services, and of which your lordship may not be aware.

"During the Burmah War Captain Chads and I both held the command of a very large force for several months—both were promoted on the same day, and both received the honour of the Order of the Bath—and, on the thanks of Government being voted in the House of Commons to the officers, and on Sir Joseph York, who was a great friend of Captain Chads, proposing that he should be particularly mentioned by name, Sir G. Cockburn rose and said that it would be the height of injustice to mention that officer without mentioning me.

"I trust the above statement will satisfy your lordship that I was not so much to blame when I drew the comparison between our respective treatment—Captain Chads having hoisted his commodore's pennant in India, having been since appointed to the *Excellent,* and lately received the good service pension ; while I have applied in vain for employment, and have met with a reception which I have not deserved.

"And now, my lord, apologizing for the length of this letter, allow me to state the chief cause of my addressing you. It is not to renew my applications for employment —for which my present state of health has totally un- fitted me—it is, that my recovery has been much retarded by a feeling that your lordship could not have departed from your usual courtesy in your reception of me as you did, if it was not that some misrepresentations of my character had been made to you. This has weighed heavily upon me ; and I entreat your lordship will let me know if such has been the case, and that you will give me an opportunity of justifying myself—which I feel assured that I can do—as I never yet have departed from the conduct of an officer and a gentleman. I am the more anxious upon this point, as, since the total wreck of West India property, I shall have little to leave my children but a good name, which, on their account, becomes doubly precious. I have the honour, &c.,

"F. MARRYAT."

I have quoted this melancholy but not altogether unmanly letter at full for the light it throws on Marryat's last years. It is clear that when the ruin of West Indian property had begun to embarrass him, he had striven to return to active service. The beginning of the letter proves that in the middle of 1847 his nerve was already gone. At last he was no longer able to bear the strain of that passion and determination of which his daughter speaks. When crossed by a First Lord of the Admiralty, with whom he could not give way to an explosion of rage, the effort required to control himself was too much for a man worn in health, and accustomed for many years past to give his feelings unchecked course. The letter may also stand as proof that Marryat's reputation as a naval officer was dear to him. As to the merits of the dispute there is no evidence to form an opinion. Lord Auckland, in a temperate letter, replied that he had no recollection of what had passed at the time, but that he certainly could have had no intention of wounding so distinguished an officer as Captain Marryat. The letter ended with the agreeable information that a good service pension had been conferred on him. Heat and disappointment on the one side, and perhaps a little dry official formality on the other—a thing which those who deal with Government officials should learn to take for granted—will doubtless account for the trouble.

From this time forward Marryat's remnant of life was filled with flights in search of health, and with every sorrow. From Wimbledon he went to Hastings, in the vain hope that a milder climate would give him a chance of recovery. For a time he seemed to improve, but it was a mere flicker. Whatever chance of recovery he had was utterly destroyed by the terrible blow which fell on him at the end of the year. His son, Lieutenant Frederick Marryat, was lost in the wreck of the *Avenger* in the Mediterranean. The *Avenger*, one of the first steamers in the

navy, was steered on a reef between Galita and the main-
land, during the night. She was under steam and sail at the
time, and struck so heavily that in a very few minutes
she was a complete wreck, with the sea breaking over her.
Frederick Marryat was below when the vessel struck. In
the confusion which followed, he was seen, by one of the
few survivors, in the waist of the ship, endeavouring to
keep the men steady, and clear away the boats. But the
Avenger broke up fast ; the funnel and mainmast fell on
the group in which Marryat stood, crushing some and
hurling others overboard, where they were swept away
in the sea that was then running. By one death or the
other he perished, and the tragedy broke his father's
heart. The young man had been wild and extravagant
—a source of expense and anxiety to his father. He had
been a midshipman of the wild type, and as a young
lieutenant had been unsettled, eager to get on shore and
find some work more agreeable and more lucrative than
a naval officer's. But if he had the faults—or rather let
us say the weaknesses—of the seaman, he also had his
finer qualities. He was a gallant and good-hearted
young fellow. A letter of his father's, written two years
or so before the wreck, speaks of him as turning up from
the China station full of life and spirit, lighting up the
house at Langham. In his then state of weakness it
must have been a killing blow to the father to hear of the
son's death, under circumstances of which no man was
better able to appreciate the horror than himself.
Marryat bore the blow stoutly, for he too had the "qualities of his defects," and as he was passionate so was he
courageous.

From Hastings, which he naturally felt had done him no good, he moved to Brighton for a month. It seemed for a moment as if the danger was past, and Dickens, among others, wrote to congratulate him on his recovery. But, in truth, the case was a hopeless one. From Brighton he returned to London for the last time to consult with the doctors. When he re-entered the outer room in which several of his family were waiting to hear the result, he had to tell them that he had been con-demned. "They say," he reported, "that in six months I shall be numbered with my forefathers." He an-nounced the decision, Mrs. Ross Church tells us, with an "undisturbed and half-smiling countenance," and we can easily believe it, for, leaving his natural bravery out of the question, life can have had no temptation for him if it was to be lived under the constant threat of such a disease as menaced him.

From London Marryat moved to Langham, and there waited for death all through the summer of 1848. It came at last through sheer weakness, and apparently with little or no pain. Ruptures of blood vessels could only be prevented by rigid abstinence from food. He speaks in the last letter he wrote—in at least the last that is printed—of living for days on lemonade till he "was reduced to a little above nothing." The illness and the remedy were alike fatal, and between the two he was gradually reduced to extinction. During the summer days he lay in the drawing-room of the house at Langham, hearing his daughters read aloud to him, till his growing weakness brought on delirium. To the last he continued to dictate pages of incoherent talk, much as Sir Walter

Scott had written mechanically long after his intellect was gone. He loved to have flowers brought him to the end. Finally, after he had long been unconscious between weakness and doses of morphia, he expired in perfect quiet just about dawn on August 9, 1848.

It ought to be unnecessary for me to add much on the character of Captain Marryat. Although our knowledge of him is fragmentary, it is my fault if enough has not been said in these pages to show what sort of man he must have been. It is tolerably clear that he was passionate, ready to think that he did well to be angry, and that anger was its own justification. Passionately eager to enjoy he must have been, and not wise in seeking enjoyment. It must be remembered, however, that he was trained in the navy in a wild time, when men repaid themselves for such hardships as the naval officer of to-day never undergoes, by excesses of which he would be incapable. Then Marryat fell into the literary and semi-literary life of London at a time when it was partly honestly, partly out of mere silly pose, dissipated and Bohemian. His wealth was the means of throwing him among a hard living set. Among them, his friends, doubtless, helped him to get rid of his money inherited and earned. He was the fast and hard living stamp of man whom the Bohemian literary gentlemen professed to admire, and he paid for his genuineness. In such a world the ardent natures wore themselves out, while the *poseur* and the humbug escaped. But if Marryat wasted his substance and hastened his death by excesses, he seems to have been generous and good to those around him. To his younger children he was kind, and if his wife fell out of his life (she is not mentioned as having been present at Langham), there is nothing to show that it was for reasons discreditable to him, or indeed to either of them. If he was one of those who are mainly their own enemies, at least he did not belong to the worst rank of a very noxious class of persons. That he was a brave man and a good officer beyond question.

As a writer Captain Marryat has never—as I began this little book by saying—been quite fairly treated. There has always been more or less a suspicion that an *Athenæum* writer, who described him as a quarter-deck captain who defied critics, and trifled with the public, writing carelessly, and not even good English, taking it for granted that the public was to read just what he chose to write, was stating the facts. He has never been recognized as one of the front rank of English novelists. Macaulay only mentions him as one among several writers on America. Carlyle's savage "slate" of him is unjust to a degree which can only be palliated by the fact that it was founded on a hasty reading of his books in the evil days after the loss of the manuscript of the French Revolution. At that time everything was looking more spectral to Carlyle than usual. Thackeray was just to him indeed, but Thackeray was exceptionally large-minded and fair. Yet I do not know what reason there is to exclude Marryat from the front rank which would not also exclude some whom we habitually put there. To rank him with Fielding, with Jane Austen, Thackeray or Richardson, would be absurd, but I see no reason why he should not stand with Smollett. He

might stand a little below him for " Humphrey Clinker's "
sake, but not very far.   Except Sir Walter Scott, no man
can be read over a longer period of life.   He may be
enjoyed at school and for ever afterwards.   I doubt
whether many boys have delighted in "Tom Jones."
Did anybody, to take the other end of life, ever
experience, on coming back to " Peter Simple " or " Mr.
Midshipman Easy," that shock which is produced by a
mature re-reading of, say, "Zanoni"?   I imagine not.
There must be a great vitality, a genuine truth, in the
writer who can stand this test, and stand is so long.   That
Marryat was to some extent a boyish writer is undeni-
able, and it seems to me to be the secret of his enduring
popularity.   His books revive in one the exact kind of
pleasure one felt in reading them in one's teens.   We
may re-read some writers who pleased then, and remember the pleasure, and regret it can be felt no longer.
Others one re-reads with ever new pleasure, but they
satisfy for reasons not felt in early days.   We see more
in them and ever more.   But with Marryat it is different.
He pleases for the same causes always, which is surely
as much as to say that he is unique of his kind.   More
than any other man he made what was written for boys
and children literature.   He was the best of his class,
and that alone entitles him to a high place.   After all, a
man can do no more than be the best of his order.
Whoever is that is surely fairly entitled to be called a
Great Writer.   Whether that title is to be grudged him
or not, he is assuredly the friend of all who read with a
simple and healthy taste.   No man has given more honest
pleasure, more wholesome stimulus to youth ; few have

given more hearty fun to older readers. If we do not think of him as "great," a word of which we might indeed be more chary than we are, at least we can think of him as kind'y, as sound, as manly—and it is possible to make a stir with one's pen and be none of those three things.

THE END.

INDEX.

BIBLIOGRAPHY.

BY

JOHN P. ANDERSON

(British Museum).

I. WORKS.

The Novels of Captain Marryat. —Percival Keene. Monsieur Violet. Rattlin the Reefer. Valerie. The author's copyright edition. 4 pts. London, Guildford [printed 1875], 8vo.

The Novels of Captain Marryat. —The Phantom Ship. The Dog Fiend. Olla Podrida. The Poacher. The author's copyright edition. London, Guildford [printed 1875], 8vo.

The Children of the New Forest. 2 vols. London [1847], 12mo. Part of a series entitled "The Juvenile Library."

——Another edition. 2 vols. London, 1849, 12mo.

——Another edition. 2 vols. London, 1850, 12mo.

——Another edition. With illustrations. London, 1853, 16mo.

A Code of Signals for the use of vessels employed in the Merchant Service. London, 1837, 8vo.

——Eighth edition. London, 1841, 8vo. The last edition edited by Captain Marryat.

——Another edition. The Universal Code of Signals, for the Mercantile Marine of all Nations, etc. London, 1854, 8vo.

——Another edition. London, 1856, 8vo.

——Another edition. London, 1861, 8vo.

——Another edition. London, 1864, 8vo.

——Another edition. London, 1866, 8vo.

——Another edition. London, 1869, 8vo.

——Another edition. London, 1879, 8vo.

A Diary in America, with remarks on its Institutions. 3 vols. London, 1839, 12mo.

——A Diary in America, with remarks on its Institutions. Part Second. 3 vols. London, 1839, 12mo.

The Floral Telegraph ; or, Affection's Signals. London [1850], 12mo.

Jacob Faithful. 3 vols. London, 1834, 12mo.

——Another edition. London, 1838, 8vo.
No. lxiii. of the " Standard Novels."

——Another edition. London, 1856, 8vo.

——Another edition. London, New York, 1873, 8vo.

——Author's edition, complete. London [1874], 8vo.

——Another edition. London, Guildford [printed 1877], 8vo.
One of a series entitled "Notable Novels."

——Another edition. London, Halifax [printed 1878], 8vo.

——Another edition. London [1881], 8vo.
One of " Ward and Lock's Standard Novels."

——Another edition. London [1883], 8vo.

Japhet in Search of a Father. 3 vols. London, 1836, 12mo.

——Another edition. London, 1838, 8vo.
No. lxiv. of the " Standard Novels."

——Another edition. London, 1856, 12mo.

——Another edition. London, 1857, 8vo.
One of the " Railway Library " series.

——Another edition. With illustrations. London, 1873, 8vo.

——Another edition. London [1881], 8vo.

——Another edition. London [1883], 8vo.

Joseph Rushbrook; or, The Poacher. 3 vols. London, 1841, 8vo.

——Another edition. 3 vols. London, 1842, 8vo.

Joseph Rushbrook ; or, The Poacher. London, 1846, 8vo.
No. civ. of the " Standard Novels."

——New edition. London, 1856, 12mo.

——New edition. London, 1857, 8vo.

——Another edition. With illustrations. London [1873], 8vo.

——Another edition. London [1880], 16mo.
One of the " Handy-Volume Marryat " series.

——Reprinted from the original edition. (A Rencontre.) London [1883], 8vo.
One of a series entitled " Notable Novels."

The King's Own. 3 vols. London, 1830, 12mo.

——Another edition. London, 1838, 8vo.
No. lxv. of the " Standard Novels."

——Another edition. London, 1856, 12mo.

——Another edition. London, 1873, 8vo.

——Another edition. London [1874], 8vo.
One of a series entitled " Notable Novels."

——Another edition. With a Memoir by Florence Marryat. Author's edition. London [1874], 8vo.

——[" Handy-Volume Marryat " edition.] London [1880], 16mo.

The Little Savage. [Edited by Frank S. Marryat.] 2 pts. London, 1848-49, 12mo.
Part of the " Juvenile Library."

——Another edition. 2 vols. London, 1850, 8vo.

——Another edition. London, 1853, 8vo.

Masterman Ready ; or, the Wreck of the Pacific. 3 vols. London, 1841, 8vo.

Masterman Ready. New edition. (*Bohn's Illustrated Library.*) London, 1851, 8vo.

——Another edition. 2 vols. London, 1853, 12mo.

——Another edition. London, 1856, 12mo.

——Another edition. (*Bell's Reading Books.*) London, 1875, 8vo.

——Another edition. London, 1878, 16mo.

——Another edition. London, 1885, 8vo.

——Another edition. With illustrations. London [1886], 8vo.

The Metropolitan : a monthly journal of literature, science, and the fine arts.
[Continued as]
The Metropolitan Magazine. Successively edited by T. Campbell, F. Marryat, etc. 57 vols. London, 1831-50, 8vo.

The Mission, or Scenes in Africa. London, 1845, 8vo.

——Another edition. London, 1853, 12mo.

——New edition. (*Bohn's Illustrated Library.*) London, 1854, 8vo.

——Another edition. London, 1856, 12mo.

——Another edition. London, 1887, 8vo.

Mr. Midshipman Easy. 3 vols. London, 1836, 12mo.

——Another edition. London. 1838, 8vo.
No. lxvi. of the "Standard Novels."

——Another edition. London, 1856, 8vo.

——Another edition. With illustrations. London, 1873, 8vo.

Mr. Midshipman Easy. Another edition. London [1879], 8vo.
One of a series entitled "Notable Novels."

——["Handy-Volume Marryat" edition.] London [1880], 16mo.

——Another edition. London, [1881], 8vo.
One of "Ward and Lock's Standard Novels."

——Another edition. London [1883], 8vo.

Narrative of the Travels and Adventures of Monsieur Violet in California, Sonora, and Western Texas. 3 vols. London, 1843, 12mo.

——Another edition. London, 1819, 8vo.

——The Travels and Adventures of Monsieur Violet among the Snake Indians and Wild Tribes of the Great Western Prairies. London, 1849, 12mo.
Vol 33 of the "Parlour Library."

——The Travels and Adventures of Monsieur Violet in California, Sonora, and Western Texas. With illustrations. London, 1874, 8vo.

——Another edition. London [1875], 8vo.

——Another edition. London [1880], 16mo.
One of the "Handy-Volume Marryat" series.

The Naval Officer ; or, Scenes and Adventures in the life of Frank Mildmay. 3 vols. London, 1829, 12mo.

——Revised edition. (*Colburn's Modern Standard Novelists*, vol. x.) London, 1839, 8vo.

——Frank Mildmay ; or, the Naval Officer, with a Memoir by Florence Marryat. London [1873], 8vo.

The Naval Officer. Another edition. London [1874], 8vo.
One of a series, entitled "Notable Novels."

——Author's edition. London [1874], 8vo.

——Another edition. London [1880], 16mo.
One of the "Handy-Volume Marryat" series.

Newton Forster; or, the Merchant Service. 3 vols. London, 1832, 12mo.

——Another edition. London, 1838, 8vo.
No. lxvii. of the "Standard Novels."

——Another edition. London, 1856, 8vo.
One of a series entitled the "Railway Library."

——Another edition. With illustrations. London, 1873, 8vo.

——Another edition. London [1874], 8vo.
One of a series entitled "Notable Novels."

——Author's edition. London [1874], 8vo.

——Another edition. London [1880], 16mo.
One of the "Handy-Volume Marryat" series.

Olla Podrida. 3 vols. London, 1840, 12mo.

——Another edition. London, 1849, 8vo.

——Another edition. London, 1856, 12mo.

——Another edition. With illustrations. London, 1874, 8vo.

——Author's copyright edition. London [1875], 8vo.

——Another edition. London [1880], 16mo.
One of the "Handy-Volume Marryat" series.

The Pacha of Many Tales. 3 vols. London, 1835, 12mo.

The Pacha of Many Tales. Another edition. Paris, 1835, 8vo.

——Another edition. London, 1838, 8vo.
No. lxviii. of the "Standard Novels."

——New edition. London, 1856, 8vo.

——Author's edition. London [1874], 8vo.

——Another edition. With illustrations. London, 1873, 8vo.

——Another edition. London [1880], 8vo.
One of the "Handy-Volume Marryat" series.

Percival Keene. 3 vols. London, 1842, 12mo.

——Another edition. London, 1848, 8vo.
No. cxiii. of the "Standard Novels."

——New edition, with a Memoir of the Author. London, 1857, 8vo.
One of the series entitled "Railway Library."

——Another edition. With illustrations. London [1873], 8vo.

——New edition. London [1875], 8vo.

——Another edition. With a Memoir of the Author. London [1880], 16mo.
One of the "Handy-Volume Marryat" series.

Peter Simple. 3 vols. London, 1834, 12mo.

——Another edition. London, 1838, 8vo.
No. lxii. of the "Standard Novels."

——Another edition. London, 1856, 8vo.

——Another edition. With illustrations. London, 1870, 8vo.

——Another edition. With illustrations. London, 1873, 8vo.

Peter Simple. Author's edition, complete. London [1874], 8vo.

——Another edition. London, Guildford [printed 1876], 8vo.

——Another edition. London, Halifax [printed 1878], 8vo.

——Another edition. London [1880], 16mo.
One of the "Handy-Volume Marryat" series.

——Another edition. London [1881], 8vo.
One of "Ward and Lock's Standard Novels."

The Phantom Ship. 3 vols. London, 1839, 12mo.

——Another edition. London, 1847, 8vo.

——Another edition. London, 1849, 8vo.

——Another edition. London, 1856, 8vo.

——Another edition. With illustrations. London, 1874, 8vo.

——Another edition. London [1880], 16mo.
One of the "Handy-Volume Marryat" series.

The Pirate and the Three Cutters. Illustrated with engravings from drawings by C. Stanfield. London, 1836, 4to.

——Another edition. With engravings by Stanfield. London, 1848, 8vo.

——New edition. (*Bohn's Illustrated Library.*) London, 1849, 8vo.

——Another edition. With a Memoir of the Author, etc. London, Beccles [printed 1877], 8vo.

——Another edition. London [1880], 8vo.

——Another edition. London [1880], 16mo.
One of the "Handy-Volume Marryat" series.

The Pirate and the Three Cutters. Another edition. With illustrations. London [1886], 8vo.

Poor Jack. With illustrations by C. Stanfield. London, 1840, 8vo.

——Another edition. London, 1880, 8vo.

——Another edition. London [1883], 8vo.
One of the series of "Notable Novels."

——Another edition. With illustrations by C. Stanfield. London, 1883, 8vo.

The Privateer's Man, one hundred years ago. 2 vols. London, 1846, 8vo.

——Another edition. London, 1853, 8vo.

——Another edition. 2 vols. London, 1854, 8vo.

——Another edition. London, 1856, 8vo.

——The Privateersman. Adventures by sea and land, in civil and savage life, one hundred years ago. (*Bohn's Illustrated Library.*) London, 1860, 8vo.

Rattlin the Reefer. London, 1838, 8vo.
No. lxix. of the "Standard Novels."

——Another edition. London, 1856, 16mo.

——Another edition. With illustrations. London, 1873, 8vo.

——Another edition. London [1875], 8vo.

——Another edition. Edited [or rather written] by Captain Marryat. ["Handy - Volume Marryat" edition.] London [1880], 16mo.

The Settlers in Canada. 2 vols. London, 1844, 8vo.

The Settlers in Canada. Another edition. London, 1854, 12mo.
——Another edition. London, 1855, 12mo.
——New edition. With illustrations by Gilbert and Dalziel. London, 1860, 8vo.
Part of "Bohn's Illustrated Library."
——Another edition. London [1856], 8vo.
——Another edition. London [1857], 8vo.
Snarleyyow; or, the Dog Fiend. 3 vols. London, 1837, 12mo.
——Another edition. Paris, 1837, 8vo.
——Another edition. London, 1847, 8vo.
No. cvii. of the "Standard Novels."
——Another edition. London, 1856, 12mo.
——The Dog Fiend; or, Snarleyyow. London, 1857, 8vo.
One of the series entitled "Railway Library."
——Another edition. With illustrations. London, New York, 1873, 8vo.
——Another edition. [Handy-volume Marryat.] London [1880], 8vo.

Suggestions for the Abolition of the present System of Impressment in the Naval Service. London, 1822, 8vo.
Valerie, an Autobiography. 2 vols. London, 1849, 12mo.
——Another edition. With illustrations. London [1873], 8vo.
——Another edition. London, 1852, 16mo.
——Author's Copyright edition. London [1875], 8vo.

Valerie, an Autobiography. Another edition. London [1880], 16mo.
One of the "Handy-volume Marryat" Series.

II. APPENDIX.

BIOGRAPHY, CRITICISM, ETC.

Cary, T. G.—Letter to a lady in France on the supposed failure of a National Bank . . . with answers to enquiries concerning the books of Captain Marryat and Mr. Dickens. Boston [U.S.], 1843, 8vo.
——Second edition. Boston [U.S.], 1844, 8vo.
Marryat, Florence. — Life and Letters of Captain Marryat. 2 vols. London, 1872, 8vo.
Marryat, Frederick.—A Reply to Captain Marryat's statements relative to the coloured West Indians, in his work entitled, "A Diary in America." [Consisting of letters which appeared in the "St. George's Chronicle."] London, 1840, 8vo.
Marshall, John. — Royal Naval Biography. 4 vols. London, 1823-35, 8vo.
Frederick Marryat, vol. iii., pp. 261-270.
Poe, Edgar A.—The Literati, etc. New York, 1850, 8vo.
Frederick Marryat, pp. 456-460.

MAGAZINE ARTICLES.

Marryat, Frederick.—New Monthly Magazine, vol. 48, 1836, pp. 228-232.—Bentley's Miscellany (with portrait), by C. Whitehead, vol. 24, 1848,

Marryat, Captain.

pp. 524-530 ; same article, Eclectic Magazine, vol. 16, 1849, pp. 135-139, and Littell's Living Age, vol. 19, pp. 540-543. — Temple Bar, vol. 37, 1873, pp. 100-106.— London Society, by T. H. S. Escott, vol. 23, 1873, pp. 31-44.
——*and his Diary.* Southern Literary Messenger, vol. 7, 1841, pp. 253-276.
——*at Langham.* Cornhill Magazine, vol. 16, 1867, pp. 149-161.
——*Life and Letters of.* Chambers's Journal, 1872, pp. 691-695.
——*Midshipman Easy.* Monthly Review, vol. 3 N.S., 1836, pp. 211-223.
——*Newton Forster.* Westminster Review, vol. 16, 1832, pp. 390-394.

Marryat, Captain.

——*Novels.* Fraser's Magazine, vol. 17, 1838, pp. 571-577.
——*Percival Keene.* Tait's Edinburgh Magazine, vol. 9 N.S., 1842, pp. 670-680.—Monthly Review, vol. 3 N.S., 1842, pp. 213-223.
——*Sea Novels.* Dublin University Magazine, vol. 47, 1856, pp. 294-308 ; same article, Eclectic Magazine, vol. 38, pp. 46-60.—Cornhill Magazine, by J. Hannay, vol. 27, 1873, pp. 170-190 ; same article, Littell's Living Age, vol. 116, pp. 676-689, and Eclectic Magazine, vol. 17 N.S., pp. 464-478.
——*Settlers in Canada.* Tait's Edinburgh Magazine, vol. 11, 1844, pp. 807, 808.
——*Snarleyyow.* Dublin University Magazine, vol. 10, 1837, pp. 325-338.

III. CHRONOLOGICAL LIST OF WORKS.

The Canterbury Poets.

EDITED BY WILLIAM SHARP.

WITH INTRODUCTORY NOTICES BY VARIOUS CONTRIBUTORS.

In SHILLING Monthly Volumes, Square 8vo. Well printed on fine toned paper, with Red-line Border, and strongly bound in Cloth. Each Volume contains from 300 to 350 pages.

Cloth, Red Edges	1s.	*Red Roan, Gilt Edges*	2s. 6d.
Cloth, Uncut Edges	1s.	*Pad. Morocco, Gilt Edges*	5s.

THE FOLLOWING VOLUMES ARE NOW READY.

CHRISTIAN YEAR.
By Rev. John Keble.
COLERIDGE. Ed. by J. Skipsey.
LONGFELLOW. Ed. by E. Hope.
CAMPBELL. Edited by J. Hogben.
SHELLEY. Edited by J. Skipsey.
WORDSWORTH.
Edited by A. J. Symington.
BLAKE. Edited by Joseph Skipsey.
WHITTIER. Edited by Eva Hope.
POE. Edited by Joseph Skipsey.
CHATTERTON.
Edited by John Richmond.
BURNS. Poems. ⎫ Edited by
BURNS. Songs. ⎭ Joseph Skipsey.
MARLOWE.
Edited by P. E. Pinkerton.
KEATS. Edited by John Hogben.
HERBERT. Edited by E. Rhys.
VICTOR HUGO.
Translated by Dean Carrington.
COWPER. Edited by Eva Hope.
SHAKESPEARE.
Songs, Poems, and Sonnets.
Edited by William Sharp.
EMERSON. Edited by W. Lewin.
SONNETS of this CENTURY.
Edited by William Sharp.
WHITMAN. Edited by E. Rhys.
SCOTT. Marmion, etc.
SCOTT. Lady of the Lake, etc.
Edited by William Sharp.
PRAED. Edited by Fred. Cooper.
HOGG. By his Daughter, Mrs Garden.
GOLDSMITH. Ed. by W. Tirebuck.
MACKAY'S LOVE LETTERS.
SPENSER. Edited by Hon. R. Noel.
CHILDREN OF THE POETS.
Edited by Eric S. Robertson.
JONSON. Edited by J. A. Symonds.
BYRON (2 Vols.)
Edited by Mathilde Blind.
THE SONNETS OF EUROPE.
Edited by S. Waddington.

RAMSAY. Ed. by J. L. Robertson.
DOBELL. Edited by Mrs. Dobell.
DAYS OF THE YEAR.
With Introduction by Wm. Sharp.
POPE. Edited by John Hogben.
HEINE. Edited by Mrs. Kroeker.
BEAUMONT & FLETCHER.
Edited by J. S. Fletcher.
BOWLES, LAMB, &c.
Edited by William Tirebuck.
EARLY ENGLISH POETRY.
Edited by H. Macaulay Fitzgibbon.
SEA MUSIC. Edited by Mrs Sharp.
HERRICK. Edited by Ernest Rhys.
BALLADES AND RONDEAUS
Edited by J. Gleeson White.
IRISH MINSTRELSY.
Edited by H. Halliday Sparling.
MILTON'S PARADISE LOST.
Edited by J. Bradshaw, M.A., LL.D.
JACOBITE BALLADS.
Edited by G. S. Macquoid.
AUSTRALIAN BALLADS.
Edited by D. B. W. Sladen, B.A.
MOORE. Edited by John Dorrian.
BORDER BALLADS.
Edited by Graham R. Tomson.
SONG-TIDE. By P. B. Marston.
ODES OF HORACE.
Translations by Sir S. de Vere, Bt.
OSSIAN. Edited by G. E. Todd.
ELFIN MUSIC. Ed. by A. Waite.
SOUTHEY. Ed. by S. R. Thompson.
CHAUCER. Edited by F. N. Paton.
POEMS OF WILD LIFE.
Edited by Chas. G. D. Roberts, M.A.
PARADISE REGAINED.
Edited by J. Bradshaw, M.A., LL.D.
CRABBE. Edited by E. Lamplough.
DORA GREENWELL.
Edited by William Dorling.
GOETHE'S FAUST.
Edited by E. Craigmyle.

London: WALTER SCOTT, 24 Warwick Lane, Paternoster Row.

GREAT WRITERS.

A NEW SERIES OF CRITICAL BIOGRAPHIES.

Edited by Professor ERIC S. ROBERTSON, M.A.

MONTHLY SHILLING VOLUMES.

VOLUMES ALREADY ISSUED—

LIFE OF LONGFELLOW. By Prof. Eric S. Robertson.
"A most readable little work."—*Liverpool Mercury.*

LIFE OF COLERIDGE. By Hall Caine.
"Brief and vigorous, written throughout with spirit and great literary skill."—*Scotsman.*

LIFE OF DICKENS. By Frank T. Marzials.
"Notwithstanding the mass of matter that has been printed relating to Dickens and his works . . . we should, until we came across this volume, have been at a loss to recommend any popular life of England's most popular novelist as being really satisfactory. The difficulty is removed by Mr. Marzials's little book."—*Athenæum.*

LIFE OF DANTE GABRIEL ROSSETTI. By J. Knight.
"Mr. Knight's picture of the great poet and painter is the fullest and best yet presented to the public."—*The Graphic.*

LIFE OF SAMUEL JOHNSON. By Colonel F. Grant.
"Colonel Grant has performed his task with diligence, sound judgment, good taste, and accuracy."—*Illustrated London News.*

LIFE OF DARWIN. By G. T. Bettany.
"Mr. G. T. Bettany's *Life of Darwin* is a sound and conscientious work."
—*Saturday Review.*

LIFE OF CHARLOTTE BRONTË. By A. Birrell.
"Those who know much of Charlotte Brontë will learn more, and those who know nothing about her will find all that is best worth learning in Mr. Birrell's pleasant book."—*St. James' Gazette.*

LIFE OF THOMAS CARLYLE. By R. Garnett, LL.D.
"This is an admirable book. Nothing could be more felicitous and fairer than the way in which he takes us through Carlyle's life and works."—*Pall Mall Gazette.*

LIFE OF ADAM SMITH. By R. B. Haldane, M.P.
"Written with a perspicuity seldom exemplified when dealing with economic science."—*Scotsman.*

LIFE OF KEATS. By W. M. Rossetti.
"Valuable for the ample information which it contains."—*Cambridge Independent.*

LIFE OF SHELLEY. By William Sharp.
"The criticisms . . . entitle this capital monograph to be ranked with the best biographies of Shelley."—*Westminster Review.*

LIFE OF SMOLLETT. By David Hannay.
"A capable record of a writer who still remains one of the great masters of the English novel."—*Saturday Review.*

LIFE OF GOLDSMITH. By Austin Dobson.
"The story of his literary and social life in London, with all its humorous and pathetic vicissitudes, is here retold, as none could tell it better."—*Daily News.*

GREAT WRITERS—*(Continued)*.

LIFE OF SCOTT. By Professor Yonge.
"For readers and lovers of the poems and novels of Sir Walter Scott, this is a most enjoyable book."—*Aberdeen Free Press.*

LIFE OF BURNS. By Professor Blackie.
"The editor certainly made a hit when he persuaded Blackie to write about Burns."—*Pall Mall Gazette.*

LIFE OF VICTOR HUGO. By Frank T. Marzials.
"Mr. Marzials's volume presents to us, in a more handy form than any English, or even French handbook gives, the summary of what, up to the moment in which we write, is known or conjectured about the life of the great poet."—*Saturday Review.*

LIFE OF EMERSON. By Richard Garnett, LL.D.
"As to the larger section of the public, to whom the series of Great Writers is addressed, no record of Emerson's life and work could be more desirable, both in breadth of treatment and lucidity of style, than Dr. Garnett's."—*Saturday Review.*

LIFE OF GOETHE. By James Sime.
"Mr. James Sime's competence as a biographer of Goethe, both in respect of knowledge of his special subject, and of German literature generally, is beyond question."—*Manchester Guardian.*

LIFE OF CONGREVE. By Edmund Gosse.
"Mr. Gosse has written an admirable and most interesting biography of a man of letters who is of particular interest to other men of letters."—*The Academy.*

LIFE OF BUNYAN. By Canon Venables.
"A most intelligent, appreciative, and valuable memoir."—*Scotsman.*

LIFE OF CRABBE. By T. E. Kebbel.
"No English poet since Shakespeare has observed certain aspects of nature and of human life more closely; and in the qualities of manliness and of sincerity he is surpassed by none. . . . Mr. Kebbel's monograph is worthy of the subject."—*Athenæum.*

LIFE OF HEINE. By William Sharp.
"This is an admirable monograph. . . . more fully written up to the level of recent knowledge and criticism of its theme than any other English work."—*Scotsman.*

LIFE OF MILL. By W. L. Courtney.
"A most sympathetic and discriminating memoir."—*Glasgow Herald.*

LIFE OF SCHILLER. By Henry W. Nevison.
"This a well-written little volume, which presents the leading facts of the poet's life in a neatly rounded picture, and gives an adequate critical estimate of each of Schiller's separate works and the effect of the whole upon literature."—*Scotsman.*

Complete Bibliography to each volume, by J. P. ANDERSON, British Museum.

Volumes are in preparation by Goldwin Smith, Frederick Wedmore, Oscar Browning, Arthur Symons, W. E. Henley, Barclay Squire, Hermann Merivale, H. E. Watts, T. W. Rolleston, Cosmo Monkhouse, Dr. Garnett, Frank T. Marzials, W. H Pollock, John Addington Symonds, etc., etc.

LIBRARY EDITION OF "GREAT WRITERS."—Printed on large paper of extra quality, in handsome binding, Demy 8vo, price 2s. 6d.

London: WALTER SCOTT, 24 Warwick Lane, Paternoster Row.